TAMING THE SLUG

CARRIE BARTLAM

Scripture Union

By the same author:
Secret never to be told - Impressions
The Magic Kingdom - Leopard books
Stranded! - Leopard books
Tricky Business - Tiger books

© Cathie Bartlam 1997
First published 1997

Scripture Union, 207–209 Queensway, Bletchley,
Milton Keynes, MK2 2EB, England.

ISBN 1 85999 054 1

British Library Cataloguing-in-Publication Data.
A catalogue record of this book is available from the British
Library.

Printed and bound in Great Britain by Cox & Wyman Ltd,
Reading.

~ 1 ~

Mel drew a line through shortbread on her piece of paper and added frozen chocolate gateau. That would be more filling and she had already got custard creams and doughnuts on the list.

'So you can all see that we've some hard work to put in before the real exams in June,' said Mr Harris. 'If you all get down to it, there's no reason, no reason at all, why you can't improve your grades in all of your subjects.'

Mel doodled on her shopping list. 'No reason!' The man was mad. Mum would freak when she saw her French and CDT marks, and her mock GCSE results in the other subjects weren't going to impress anyone – well, not in her family. Mr Harris had been quite con-gratulatory – even an 'A' in English, but it wasn't his praises that Mel longed for.

Maybe toffee crunch ice cream would be nicer than vanilla. As the rain hurled itself at the classroom window, like a three year old having a tantrum, Mel's thoughts escaped back to tonight's party, away from the mock results that seemed to dance in front of her eyes. Last time she had bought that creamy yoghurt that was on special offer but tonight she fancied something more solid. Maybe a fruit pie or a cheesecake? She'd have to see how much money she had left from her ten pounds. A surge of excitement went through her. Thinking about tonight was what kept her going, as all around her classmates discussed their results, chattering like gossips in a newsagent's.

'Hey, you, under there,' Sarah pulled back the curtain of long brown hair that hid Mel's pale face. 'Not bad, eh?'

'Suppose.'

'Suppose! Honestly, Melanie Chambers, you're the limit. You've got A to C in all subjects ...'

'Except French and CDT.'

'Well, you hate French, and haven't you been listening? We're all getting extra help for CDT. If I'd got your results I'd be dancing on the moon.' Sarah could have shook her best friend, who seemed to have as much life and fun in her these days as an over-stuffed cushion.

'Go and dance, then.' Mel attempted a smile, which didn't reach her clear green eyes.

'I will, don't worry.' Sarah paused. 'What are you writing?' She grabbed the list. 'Grief, calories or what?'

'My cousins.'

'Cousins?'

'They're coming for tea. Mum asked me to get some treats for them on the way home.'

Sarah looked puzzled. 'I've never heard you talk about cousins before.'

Mel thought rapidly. 'Well, they're children of a friend of Mum's, little, about eight, not real cousins but like them.'

4

'I'll come to the supermarket with you on the way home, after the next lesson. I'll see you by the front gate.'

'See you,' Mel agreed, her mind racing as the bell sounded for the last period of the day. No way was she shopping with Sarah. That was her treat, her special part of the day.

Leaving school by the rear exit, Mel half ran to the small supermarket that lay in the opposite direction to home. As she slowly investigated the aisles of food, a calm peace began to spread over her, like softened butter. It was going to be fine.

Rum and raisin ice cream was on special offer, but not as nice as toffee crunch, so Mel treated herself to the latter. At the check-out she managed to cram her purchases into a rucksack, refusing repeated offers of a carrier bag bearing the store's name.

Tired, relieved, wet through and content, Mel walked home, the edge of the gateau box sticking painfully into her back. Not much longer now, just a few hours, but first she had to tell them about her results.

As she put the key into the front door lock Mel could hear her mum talking in her loud telephone voice. Mel had forgotten that it was one of her half-days at the solicitor's, where she worked as a legal secretary. It made hiding the rucksack that much more difficult.

She paused and listened, which wasn't hard. Mum was on her favourite subject. Caro. Caroline Elizabeth Chambers, age twenty-one, destined for a First at Oxford in Physics! Elder sister of Mel, age fifteen, destined to be an also-ran for the rest of her life.

'It was lovely to have her home for the vacation ... yes, she's gone back now ... I must show you the photos of the ball she went to ... You're right, stunning ...,' a girlish giggle,' I don't know who she gets it from, not me or her father, that's for sure.' A longer silence. 'Well, obviously there's been no difficulty with her getting funding for her doctorate. Gloria, I need to go, I think Melanie's just come home, um, yes, shame, you're right, a shame. Bye.'

Shame, thought Mel, she's talking about me again, must be. I'll never be like Caroline. I still don't really know what Physics is and who will ever call me stunning? At the same time she called 'Hello, Mum,' in a bright voice.

'Hello, darling. My, what have you got in that rucksack?'

'You sound like someone out of an American soap opera,' joked Mel. 'Just books,' and she rushed upstairs and thrust the offending rucksack into the back of the wardrobe.

That was a close shave. Mel had known Mum rummage through her bag for rubbish enough times to make her wary. She got changed out of her uniform. How she hated her stomach. Her black leggings emphasised her slight curve before she hid the horrible sight under a baggy jumper. Time for a few sit-ups before tea.

Mum barged in. 'I nearly forgot,' she said. 'Didn't you get your results today?'

Mel heaved herself upright, her face red with exertion, her heart racing. She'd have to tell her. She couldn't get the piece of paper out of the hidden rucksack. Slowly she recited the results, starting with the A in English and finishing with E for French. As she spoke, Mum's permanently worried frown got deeper and by the end of the recital she looked a lot older than her late forties.

'E! E!' she screeched, before deliberately dropping her

voice an octave. 'No daughter of mine has ever got an E, in fact no daughter has ever got lower than a B, and that was when she was ill.'

Mel's insides knotted up. Mum could be very Victorian and melodramatic, but these calm tirades were terrible. 'Daughters of mine!' What rot! There was only her and Caroline. What she really meant was that Caroline was brilliant and she was thick.

'So, I expect you to work, every evening, two or three hours and to get those grades up.'

'Yes, Mum.' Mel stood quiet and passive.

'When I think of all the opportunities you've had, you and Caro, all those things you take for granted and now this, E for French! And here's me, had to leave school at fifteen, none of your privileges, my girl, working my way up to secretary, trying to do 'A' levels at my age, while you throw away everything you've ever been given. I'm disappointed, Mel, really disappointed, and to think what a good girl you've always been.'

'Yes, Mum, er, no.' Mel wasn't sure of the appropriate response.

'We'll see what Dad says at tea.' Mum stormed off, her exit from the bedroom spoiled when her lambswool cardigan caught on the door handle.

Tea was awful. Mum was angry yet trying to be calm and reasonable but failing. Dad was on nights at the car factory so it felt like breakfast time to him and Granny was confused by it all. She lived in two rooms that had been built above the garage in what was grandly called the granny flat and joined the family for their main meals.

'So,' said Dad, 'you got a good smattering of Bs and Cs.'

'Good smattering! Andrew, what about French and CDT?'

7

'Janet, she's never liked them.'

There they go again, thought Mel, talking about me as if I don't exist.

'And whose fault is that? I've told you many times we should have found the money from somewhere for private tuition.'

'Our Caroline did all right,' replied Dad, under the cover of his rubbery lasagne.

But I'm not Caroline, Mel wanted to shout, but instead kept her eyes downcast as she toyed with her salad.

'You're too hard on that girl,' Granny said. 'Always have been. E sounds good to me. I never got one.'

'Mother, shut up,' Janet glared at her mother. 'You don't understand. Education is everything.'

'Why?' Granny dripped cheese sauce on her none-too-clean thick floral dress and looked stubborn.

Mum got up. 'It gives choices, that's why. I don't want any daughter of mine to get stuck in a job she hates just because she hasn't got an education.'

'Well, your job is okay,' said Granny, dabbing her dress with a grey hanky. 'Why you want to do these 'A' levels is beyond me. Husband and family were good enough for me.'

'But not me,' said Janet slowly, 'and not my daughters.'

Mel hated it. They made her sound like a possession, my daughters, something to boast about, like the new CD player, a belonging, not a person. No one asked what she thought and felt. No one was bothered.

'Talking about family, Granny, did I tell you I've heard from one of the Chambers in New Zealand. He thinks he is related to great grandfather Albert, and I think he might be right. I'll check it tomorrow on my chart.' Dad's family tree chart was pinned up in the kitchen, much to Mum's annoyance, as it clashed with her ideas of interior design.

At last the meal ended. Dad went off to work, muttering something about some ancestor in 1857 who had fourteen children and didn't bother about GCSEs. Mum collected her books for her Psychology class. Mel thought it ironic. Here was Mum learning about what made people tick and she hadn't a clue as far as Mel was concerned. She washed up with Granny.

'Are you going to watch telly with me, Mel love?' she said, wiping down the already near sterile surfaces of the kitchen.

'Just *Eastenders*.' Mel loved Granny's shabby, over-crowded living-room where Mum was never allowed to hoover or dust. 'Then I've got to study.'

Granny gave her a hug. 'Don't you worry too much about it all. You'll do fine. We can't all be like Caroline, thank goodness.'

Mel wasn't sure if she had heard the last two words correctly. She knew she loved Granny though. 'I must do some work, Granny,' but already she was eagerly await-ing those moments when she could get to the rucksack. Dad at work, Mum at her class and Granny dozing by her television. Yes, not long now until it would be safe. She felt dizzy with expectation.

~ 2 ~

At last *Eastenders* finished, and with mounting excitement Mel escaped to her room. She had about ninety minutes, plenty of time. Rescuing the rucksack from the wardrobe, she poured the contents out onto her bed. The ice-cream had started to melt and a toffee-coloured stain splashed over her exercise books. No time for that now, she could clean the books later.

Mel laid her goodies on the bed, making herself wait just one more moment. She rushed downstairs. Experience had taught her that a litre of orange squash made it easier later on. She felt great, her whole life was compressed into the contents of the bed as she became unaware of anything else. The excitement threatened to overwhelm her and Mel wanted to jump up and down and clap her hands together. So she did. And then she began.

With a sigh of ecstasy she launched straight into the gateau, tearing huge chunks off with her bare hands and stuffing them straight into her mouth. The cream was soft, while the inside of the cake was still frozen hard; the contrast was wonderful. A roaring voice inside her screamed, 'Fill me! Give me!'

Both hands lunged at the doughnuts, and she took alternative bites from them, washing them down with great gulps of sticky orange squash. Unaware that brown and yellow rivulets were dribbling from her mouth, Mel attacked the custard creams, but their dryness irritated her. Scooping handfuls of toffee crunch ice cream, she rammed that into her mouth until only the black cherry fruit pie was left.

All the pain and confusion in her life was obliterated as she savoured the crisp thick pastry and spurting filling. It was all right. Everything was fine. Nothing mattered. The roaring lion was satisfied, asleep, not needing another feed for a few days.

Mel felt warm and loved, as if she had been wrapped in a great big soft duvet and snuggled in the safest place on earth. The raging desire had gone, replaced by a tremendous feeling of quiet contentment. Mel was happy, the lull before the storm had happened, as usual.

Feeling great lasted just a few minutes. As if waking from a deep trance, Mel sat upright and looked around her, suddenly aware of what was going on.

'Oh, God,' she muttered. 'Not again. No!' Like cries of pain from a wounded animal, the words escaped. 'No! You disgusting creature, you pig, you idiot.'

Panic started to set in as she pulled up her jumper and saw her swollen stomach, getting more bloated every second. It would swell until it burst, splashing its ghastly contents over the pretty pink and green room. Or worse, she'd be fat, huge, obese, fatter than ever, like a lumbering cart-horse in a world of sleek thoroughbreds.

There was no time to lose. Only about half an hour left. Mel ran for the bathroom and began the familiar routine. Like an automaton she turned on the shower before kneeling by the loo. Sticking two fingers down her throat, she made herself sick. Mel watched as undigested chunks of food returned to the surface. Flushing the loo repeatedly, she waited until all that was being vomited was brown and cream goo, the chocolate gateau that she had started with.

Nearly over. Exhausted, Mel ran cold water into her squash bottle. Only a few more heaves. Drinking down the clean water, past her raw throat, she forced herself to spew up the liquid until it ran clear.

It was okay. It had all gone. No food remained in her body to contaminate her with its excess calories. All the fat and carbohydrates, thousands of calories, had gone, disappeared without a trace. Her huge stomach had shrunk back to normal. It didn't matter that Mel was exhausted, a cold sweat making her feel clammy, and that her stomach and upper chest felt as if she'd been stamped on. None of it mattered. It was all over.

Relief made Mel weak with gratitude. No one had interrupted her. The ritual was nearly over. She sloshed great blobs of toilet cleanser round the bowl and poured wild apricot shower gel liberally around the bath, as the shower still beat its wasteful insistent rhythm. The vile smell of vomit was replaced by the over-sweet odour of competing pine disinfectant and shower gel; it was okay.

'I must hurry,' said Mel. 'Mum will be back soon.'

She washed her face, sponged the front of her jumper and sped back to her room.

Disgust threatened to choke her as she surveyed the scene. Wrappers, the ripped gateau box, spilt squash and melted toffee ice cream oozing out of its pot, rioted together on her pretty flowery duvet. Mel stuffed all the rubbish into a carrier bag. It hadn't been as bad as this before. She'd never messed up the bed. Tearing the duvet cover off, she dabbed at the stain that had seeped through to the actual duvet. What would Mum say? Quickly Mel ran downstairs and put duvet and cover into the washing machine and left them churning together as if in a locked embrace, hiding her secret.

The door opened. It was Mum. Mel jumped guiltily. Mum wasn't due back yet.

'What's this? Are you doing the washing?'

'I spilt orange all over my duvet, while I was working. You know how it stains, so I thought I'd better wash it now.' Well, it was a half-truth. Grief, she had said she had been working! What about the toffee ice-cream on her exercise books? What if Mum asked to see what she had done that evening?

Mel need not have worried. Mum was impressed with Mel's activities with the washing machine.

'You had better take Caroline's duvet. These take days to dry out, and Mel, be more careful in future. Anyway, what have you been doing?'

'I watched telly with Granny.' That always got Mel one or two good points. 'And then I went in my room until I knocked the squash over.'

Mum put the kettle on. 'Well, let's have a cup of tea. You deserve a break if you've been working until now. There's a bit of carrot cake left if you would like some.'

Mel felt her stomach heave. 'No thanks.'

Mum smiled. 'You're right. Me neither. I never seem to shift this extra stone I carry around with me. How I came to have a daughter as slim as Caroline I don't know, and with curves in all the right places.'

But not a daughter as slim as me! thought Mel, desperate to escape from Mum's idea of a cosy chat over a pot of tea. She'd still got the rubbish to deal with. What if Mum followed her up to her room and saw the carrier bag? Mel looked at her as if she was seeing a stranger for the first time. Smart, expensive clothes that were slightly old-fashioned but would never date that much: well-cut tartan skirt, ruffled linen blouse, toning lambswool cardigan, even her mock pearl necklace and real pearl earrings, just to go to night school. Mel wondered what the other students made of her. She wondered what she thought of her mother.

'I decided not to go for coffee with the girls afterwards tonight,' said Mum. 'I need to get on with my reading for our next assignment. Mrs Stirch said that if I get this 'A' level, and I should, I could try for an access course for university.'

'To do what?'

'Perhaps teaching, or maybe law. I'm not sure yet.'

Mel hoped that Janet Chambers would never be inflicted on the unwilling world of schoolchildren. They would never have a moment's peace.

'If only I'd had the chances you girls have. She,' Mum nodded vigorously in the direction of Granny's room, 'couldn't see the point in it when jobs were so easy to come by. Even though I wanted to stay on at school, she wouldn't hear of it.' Mum failed to add that her widowed mother was struggling to bring up four children on her own. 'So, you know what I always say ...' she paused and Mel waited for today's cliché, 'God helps them that helps themselves.'

Mel grasped this as a cue to leave. 'Talking of which, I'll do another hour before bed, but I'll take Benjy,' Mel pointed to the snoring spaniel, 'for a quick walk first.'

'It's raining,' protested Mum.

'I won't be long. He's getting fat.' Like me, she added silently. 'I'll borrow Dad's kagoul.'

The voluminous waterproof easily hid the carrier bag in its folds. Mel had some difficulty getting a lead on playful Benjy without dropping the bag on the floor in front of Mum. She looked as if she would be sitting at the kitchen table reading her books for hours.

'Mel, what did you say spilt on your duvet?'

'Squash.'

'That water looks a mighty funny colour. I hope the dye's not coming out of the cover. It's very brown.'

'It'll be all right when it gets to rinse.' Mel rushed out of the door, away from the accusing, diluted, chocolate foamy turbulence of the washing machine.

Slowly she walked along the well-lit roads, not noticing the rain, as Benjy sniffed at every lamppost and street corner. At last she got to the park entrance and left the carrier bag and its evidence in the huge litter bin.

Finally over. All gone. Mel felt pleased and disgusted with herself, at the same time. She was worn out with the evening's activities, but it had been a success. The lion had been satisfied, the great aching hole had been filled and she had got rid of all the food. But it was awful.

'I've got to stop,' said Mel to Benjy, who ignored her. 'I can't go on like this.' The rain slowed down and a brief gap in the clouds gave her a glimpse of the pure moon. Mel looked up. 'God,' she said, 'This is awful. I hate it, but I can't stop it. Do something.' But what could he do, this God she heard about at church, who was to be praised and worshipped, who she wanted to follow? What could he do about a tired, confused, fifteen-year-old girl who had a dreadful secret, who stuffed herself silly and then vomited it all up?

Mel sighed. She would just have to stop it on her own. 'But I don't want to,' she said, as she walked Benjy back to the house. 'How can I?'

15

~ 3 ~

Mel woke to the sound of the washing machine reaching its final rinse and spin. Something had got stuck in it again and it sounded terrible. The bedroom door suddenly flew open.

'Mel, school.' Mum was ready for work. 'Dad'll be in soon. Ask him to have another look at that machine. I don't know what's in orange squash nowadays but that stain didn't come out first time. I didn't realise they put brown colouring in it.'

'Nor me,' muttered Mel.

'Anyway, I am not buying that brand again. In fact, pure fruit juice and water from now on. Oh, by the way, I'll pick you up a French revision book on the way back from work.'

'Mum, I'd like to drop French.'

'Drop French! Don't be so silly. You just need to get down to learning it properly.' She went out, calling goodbye and getting Mel to promise to hang up the duvet.

16

Mel went through the motions of getting ready for school. First, however, she had to weigh herself again. Horrors, the scale was up by half a kilo, not down, as was usual in the morning. She'd weigh herself again later. The scales made her even more determined to fast today, eat nothing, to start to make up for yesterday's binge. That way, if any gross calories had got into her digestive system, they would be cancelled out. Anyway she felt awful, and her stomach revolted at the thought of any onslaught. She put her packed lunch in her rucksack. She would throw it away. Through the sandwich box lid she could see the wholemeal bread, sticks of carrot and celery and fruit. That meant Mum was on one of her diets again. Sure enough, stuck discreetly on the inside of a cupboard door was the latest diet plan, complete with squares to colour in for each pound lost. Mel had seen it all before. Mum looked fine to her, for a Mum. If she thought she was fat, what did that make Mel?

Just before she left, Dad came in from work. He looked grey. He hated night shifts. In fact the only good thing about them was that Janet, his wife, didn't expect him to go fitness training when he had been up all night.

'I reckon that Chambers from New Zealand is related,' he said, collapsing at the table. 'Seems he was born near Chipping Sodbury. I'll have to look at the parish records. Do you want to come, Mel?'

'Now?'

'No, you dafty, Saturday.'

Mel had spent more weekends in record offices and freezing cold country churches than she could remember. In terms of interest value it lay somewhere between French revision and cleaning her room.

'I'd better study, Dad.'

'Suppose you're right. Never mind, I'll take your Gran. Likes a trip out, she does.' He looked at Mel. 'Are you okay? You look a bit pale. Your throat sounds sore. Are you getting a cold?'

Mel's throat ached from being sick so much. Dad mustn't guess. 'I'm fine, Dad. Oh, can you have a look at the washing machine? It's playing up again.' Mel's arms were full of wet duvet. 'Where shall I put this?'

'Try the bath, put a rack over it. Here, leave it on the table, I'll sort it out later. Now I wonder whether to pop down the motorway to Chipping Sodbury or take the scenic route.' He got his road atlas out and Mel slipped quietly off to school, not envying Granny's planned Saturday outing at all.

Sarah was waiting at the post box, as usual.

'What happened to you last night?'

'Last night?'

'Going shopping, the cousins. I waited for ages.'

Mel had forgotten all about the imaginary family friends. 'I must have missed you, I'm sorry.'

Sarah shrugged. 'Okay. Did you have a good time?'

'All right,' Mel improvised. 'You know what it's like with little kids. They are into everything.'

'And your mum doesn't like the house messed up, does she?'

Sarah hardly ever went to Mel's home. She felt that if she disturbed as much as a carefully arranged cushion, Mel's mum would tut-tut it back into place. It looked like something out of a magazine, the glossy sort, apart from Granny's room which was wonderfully cluttered and where she had once written her name in the dust and found it still there weeks later.

Mel giggled. 'Not like your home, is it?' She had to get

18

the conversation off the non-existent party and children. 'I love it at yours.'

'Well, Mum says trying to keep the place tidy with three kids, two dogs, no Dad, a full-time job and our Kevin who takes bikes to bits in the house, is like clearing snow in a blizzard. Pointless. Do you know, I found those slouch socks, the green ones I had for Christmas, still with their wrapping paper, down the back of the fridge yesterday. Fridge, I ask you!' Sarah wasn't bothered by the Phipps' family domestic arrangements. 'They were covered in dust and yoghurt.'

'Yoghurt?'

'Someone, our Kevin probably, had spilt it on top of the fridge and it had dripped everywhere.'

Mel smiled. No way could she imagine her mum surviving in such a house. She freaked out at Granny's rooms and rarely went in them, as the shock to her system was too much.

School ground slowly through its usual motions. Four double periods. Each subject teacher held forth on the need to work hard for GCSEs. 'A' level choices were discussed. By now, those who wanted to go into the Sixth Form College attached to Plumpton Park were supposed to have provisionally chosen their subjects. Apart from English, Mel hadn't a clue what she wanted to do, a fact which had not escaped her form tutor, Mr Harris. She had to see him at lunch time.

'Well, Mel,' he said, deliberately rhyming the words, and smiling at her, like a spider welcoming a fly into its lair. 'So it's English and what?'

'I'm not sure, Sir.'

'I suggest you don't go for languages. Your French, how shall we put it, leaves something to be desired. I'm surprised you did it really. Most of the other students are

19

doing a maximum of eight subjects. You appear to be doing ten.'

'Extra music, as well, Sir.' Mel took her courage in her hands. She had tried in vain to get her parents, her Mum, to understand that eight subjects were plenty for her. But, oh no, Caroline had done ten, easily, and now look at her. The school was happy to let bright pupils do extra, and Mel must not miss the opportunity. Mel hated the opportunity, but no one ever listened to her, so she had packed her thoughts and feelings into a tight bundle and hidden them deep inside herself. The good, compliant schoolgirl had to be a credit to her family and school. But it wasn't working.

'Sir, I'd like to drop French and Music or CDT.' There, she'd said it. Mel dared not look at Mr Harris, so she sat gazing at her lap, convinced her stomach was bulging over her skirt waistband.

'That sounds like a good idea,' Mel was so surprised she looked straight at the teacher. 'I think CDT will be fine. You're all going to get extra help with that, so I'd cut the French and the Music. You'll get to University with eight good results, and 'A' levels, of course. It might not be Oxford, like Caroline though.'

Mel's pleasure at his understanding of her predicament was whipped away from her. Always Caroline, the first girl from the Comprehensive to go to Oxford, and to do a science. Physics! Who got top grades in all her exams, who was the star of Plumpton Park, who was her sister, her clever, beautiful, talented sister. Who, said a little voice, she wished had never been born.

'So I'll see your French and Music teachers, Mel, and I'm sure I can leave it to you to discuss your decision with your parents. We'll think about 'A' level subjects another time, okay?'

'Yes, Sir, thank you.'

Mel rejoined her friends for lunch. So far she hadn't made it to the park litter bin, not with Sarah waiting for her. Her lunch box seemed to grow bigger and bigger in her bag, but she mustn't eat its contents.

'Have you got your sandwiches?' asked Sarah. 'We kept you a place. Move up a bit, Tina.'

Mel squeezed in the gap between Tina and Liz. 'I've eaten,' she said, 'before I saw old Harris.' Lying was becoming easier the more she did it, although twinges of guilt, like toothache, still hit her. As a Christian she knew lying wasn't on, but what could she do? She could hardly say that she had eaten ten pounds' worth of food last night and sicked it all up, so she had to fast today. Maybe the best thing to do was not to say much at all.

'What did Harris want?' asked Tina.

'Oh, 'A' levels and stuff. He says I can drop French and Music and concentrate on the other subjects.'

'Your mum will be pleased!' said Sarah, as Mel tried to send her a look to shut her up. 'Me, I'm not going to think about next year until the summer.'

'You'll have to,' said Tina, 'if you want to go on a course.'

'Just 'cos you've got life sussed out, Tina, doesn't mean I have,' said Sarah.

'I've always wanted to work with babies and children. I can work at the nursery, as an assistant, and then do my NNEB,' explained Tina.

'Before you get married and have lots of babies of your own,' said Sarah.

'And what's wrong with that?' Tina got defensive. 'We can't all be brainy, like the brilliant Chambers sisters.'

'I'm not brainy,' protested Mel, but no one listened. 'Liz is cleverer than me.' She hated her friends thinking she was a know-it-all, especially as it wasn't true.

'But hardly Oxford material!' said Liz, a big jolly girl with a gloriously clear complexion. She was far more interested in her latest boyfriend, Pete, than in her future. 'Do you know, Pete's taking me ski-ing at the weekend.'

'Oh, yeah. Switzerland?' said Sarah. 'How romantic.'

'Well, actually, it's a dry ski slope near the centre of Birmingham. But it's still ski-ing.'

'How exotic. Can we all come?' teased Sarah.

'Get lost.' Liz yawned and stretched as lunch break ended. 'It'd be very romantic with you lot.'

'Hope you break a leg!' Tina got in a parting shot. She turned to Mel. 'Are you doing anything tonight?'

'I've got to study.'

'Oh, well, see you.' The girls split up for the afternoon.

Mel went through the rest of the day desperately working out how to tell Mum about the French and Music. She decided to write her a note and to give it to her after tea. Mel had been so nervous about the note at tea time that she had forgotten about the fast and now felt terribly guilty at having eaten one of Granny's beef stews with a suet dumpling. The scales had crept up another half kilo and Mel wished she was miles away. She started running on the spot, wondering if Mum would react to the note.

She didn't have long to wonder.

'Melanie!' The screech could have been heard a block away. 'What's this nonsense?' Heavy feet pounded up the stairs.

'Mum, I ...'

'Mum, nothing! I don't know what you are thinking of. All that's the matter with you, my girl, is that you are far too lazy for your own good.'

22

'It's not. I can't do them.' Mel protested.

'Can't! Won't, more likely. A couple of poor results and we have this reaction. You just need to buckle down and work hard. Do you hear me?'

'Yes, Mum.' It was hopeless.

Mum took a deep breath and with a great effort calmly said, 'I'll help you with a study timetable and we can check your vocabulary together. Don't you worry, this is just a little phase you're going through. I'm sorry I shouted, Mel, but we never had this with Caro. However, I accept that shouting doesn't achieve anything.'

'No, Mum.'

'So, no more talk of dropping subjects. Now, you make a plan and I'll check it later. Okay?'

'Yes, Mum.' But it wasn't okay. Why hadn't she listened to her? Was it so awful not to do ten GCSEs? Mel wanted to cry but couldn't. She wanted to scream and yell, but she mustn't. Most of all she wanted to bury herself and her bleeding feelings into the biggest gooey cake in the world and be smothered by its comforting embrace.

~ 4 ~

Mel was woken from a deep sleep by Mum's arrival with a cup of tea.

'I thought you could work on your vocab before school. I'll test you then over breakfast.' She dropped a French revision book on the snuggled heap that was Mel. 'Start at the beginning. I'll take Benjy out. I'll be back soon.'

Groaning, Mel rolled over. Seven o'clock, no light from outside penetrating through the gap in the curtains. Seven o'clock! This was ridiculous. Mum was nuts. I bet Dad would stop her, thought Mel, if he wasn't on nights. What's she trying to prove? Reluctantly she sat up and sipped the rapidly cooling tea and stared at the page in front of her. Mum didn't realise that it wasn't just the words that were her problem, it was how they went together, and where to put the verbs. Still, if it got Mum off her back, Mel would go through the motions.

Forty-five minutes later Mum and Mel shared breakfast, which was unusual, in that most mornings Mel just grabbed something to eat on her way out. Mum had made an effort, Mel had to admit. The table was set nicely, with a few sprigs of brave yellow winter jasmine brightening up the scene.

'There's far too much fat in dairy products,' Mum began, producing a carton of soya milk. 'So we'll try this.'

Mel refused and ate her cornflakes dry, followed by toast with no butter, just marmalade. Meanwhile Mum tested her on the names of buildings and parts of the body. Mel complied, going through the ritual of question and answer, while inwardly seething. No one would have guessed that at that moment she would have cheerfully throttled her mother.

If she thinks I'm doing this every day, thought Mel, she's got another thing coming. She twisted strands of long straight hair round her fingers until she had tied her left hand into knots. Then she slowly undid them.

'Stop fiddling! Honestly, Mel, at times you are like a child.'

Wish I was, thought Mel, or old enough to get away from here.

'You'll be bald by the time you're thirty!'

Briefly Mel toyed with the idea of dyeing her hair orange or pink or something. That would really give Mum something to moan about. But I haven't got the guts, she thought. I can't stand up to her about French, or anything. What's the point of doing something daft like dyeing my hair? I'll only make a mess of it. Oh, heck, I've eaten my breakfast, I said I wouldn't. That's another, what, five or six hundred calories.

'Where's your sandwich box? Your lunch is ready.'

'Thanks, Mum. I'll get it in a moment.' Help! Two days' lunches to get rid of. 'Doesn't your bus go soon?'

Mum rushed off, leaving Mel to clear up. It was still too early to go to school, but she couldn't face Dad and his family tree, so she set off for school via the park, where she dumped her lunches. Okay, so I'll be starving by tonight, she thought, but I mustn't get fat, well, fatter.

First double period was games. Netball in the freezing cold on a grey miserable day. Mel changed into her kit, her back to the class so no one could see her thirty-six inch bust or notice that her gym skirt was size twelve to fourteen. Her thighs repelled her. Great pale telegraph poles, expanding every day. She'd have to try the bin bag trick again tonight, although trying to sleep with the bin bags tied round her legs was nearly impossible. Still if she sweated off even a centimetre it was worth it.

'What are you doing, screwed up in the corner?' It was Sarah, no inhibitions, down to her pants and bra, who had crept up to her, her hands outstretched, ready to tickle her.

Mel flinched away. If Sarah touched her she'd feel how fat she was.

'Getting ready for netball. I hope I can be centre.'

'Why?'

'I like running around, to keep warm.' To burn up the calories, more like, added Mel silently.

'I suppose you've got a point. Anyway, I missed you again at the post box.'

'I left early.' Mel wanted to tell Sarah about the dire breakfast sesssion with Mum, but it sounded so stupid. Sarah would laugh and tell her to stop her mum being so pushy. Anyway, Mum meant well, Mel felt a sudden flash of family loyalty, even though she envied Sarah, whose Mum didn't seem to know homework existed.

'Well, wait for me tomorrow.' Sarah laughed. 'I've learned the posting times by heart, now!'

Mel got her wish to run round like a playful puppy, and with about as much skill.

'Try throwing the ball at me, not over my head,' called Tina, as goal shooter. Stupid girl was good at games. It must have been all that playing with little kids, developing, what did she call it, hand and eye co-ordination. She'd have the toddlers in her nursery circuit training, if she could.

'You'll never make the team,' said Liz, puffing past her in a vain effort to catch a glimpse of Pete, who was in the Lower Sixth, and playing football on a nearby pitch.

'Don't want to,' grumbled Mel, trying to work out if she'd burnt off the toast and marmalade yet.

'Of course you do, like Caroline,' Liz said carelessly. 'Doesn't Pete look gorgeous, all muddy and sweaty?'

'Suppose,' said Mel, seething. That sister again! It was bad enough seeing the framed photo out of the paper in the school entrance hall every day: '*Caroline Chambers, captain of Plumpton Park under-sixteens netball team, receives this year's County Championship Trophy*,' without her so-called friends rubbing it in.

'Suppose! He's perfect.' Liz persisted. 'Don't you fancy anyone?'

Mel zoomed off after the ball, to get away. Fancy anyone? What was the point? No one would look at her, anyway. Why daydream over lads who didn't know she existed, even if they were really cool, like Daniel and Steve, in the Sixth Form, or Mark at church. It was far safer to fantasise secretly over blokes on the television than risk the real thing. And now Liz was crazy about Pete, when last summer it had been Paul who was gorgeous. Mel could well remember the hysterics when that hadn't worked out.

Sweaty, rain-splashed and tired, the girls crammed into the showers. Mel loathed this part of the week more than anything. She'd tried hiding in the loo and getting changed in there but Miss Parker was wise to that trick. The gym teacher made them all shower, whether they liked it or not, unless they had a period. She'd quickly realised that Mel was unlikely to be in that condition three weeks out of four.

Sarah pranced around as usual, splashing everyone, and scenting the air with cloying rose shower gel.

'Wish I'd got hips like yours,' said Tina, as she danced past.

'You can have them.'

'Seriously, I read that it's better for childbirth to have big, I mean, good hips. Mine are non-existent.' Tina explained.

'And mine are? Existent, I mean.' Sarah grinned. 'Well, I'm not having children, ever.'

'How can you say that?'

'Quite easily. Anyway, Tina, what are you going to do when you've had all these babies?'

'Foster. Adopt. Run a home. I'll think of something.'

'I wonder what Pete thinks about children?' mooned Liz.

Sarah wasn't amused. 'You're nuts. Sixteen and thinking about children.'

'Not for years, Sarah. Anyway, I don't want to end up like one of those shapeless women, with rolls of fat, who lie on the beach in the summer looking as if they need ironing.' Liz towelled her flat stomach dry. 'It's funny how we're all different shapes, different heights.'

'Different brains!' added Tina, struggling into her tights.

'Like there's me, sort of curvy,' said Liz, warming to her theme, 'and Sarah's, well ...'

'Cuddly,' laughed Sarah. 'Warm-hearted, caring and cuddly.'

'And Tina is slim,' added Liz. 'And we all wish we could be like Mel, tall, willowy. My Mum says she should be a model.'

Mel was flabbergasted. 'Tall, willowy.' They were mad. Couldn't they see her elephant thighs and great curving stomach, to say nothing of her bum, which fortunately she could hardly ever see? They were liars, all of them. Angrily she finished getting dressed and, with hardly a word, followed the others to double English.

By teatime Mel was so hungry she felt faint. She wanted to fall onto the shop-bought meat pie, but made herself eat slowly, and leave her potatoes.

'You'll be like a bird,' warned Granny, who was tired. Her arthritis was playing her up after she had been out all day on some pensioners' trip, organised by the church.

'I'll fly away then,' joked Mel. 'Soar into the sky! Seriously, Granny, I'm full.' But she wasn't. The lion inside was starting to stir from its deep sleep, to twitch around, and growl softly. Mel shut it up, temporarily, with a bowl of fresh fruit salad. It took all her self-control not to finish off the food on the plates as she washed up. Mum was at home tonight so no way could Mel binge, and in any case she hadn't got the food.

'God, help, don't let me do it tonight,' Mel called out loud, as she got her study books together. 'Stop me!' But even as she said it another part of her was longing to eat away the turmoil inside.

The noise from Granny's television reached her. With a supreme effort of her will, Mel took her books into Granny's room.

'Is it all right if I study in here tonight, Granny? I can keep you company.'

'Course, darling, I'll turn the telly off.'

'I can work with it on.' Mel squatted on the only free patch of carpet space and pulled one of the coffee tables up to her. Removing a dying plant, a silver-framed photo of a long-dead Grandad, two china figures of a Victorian boy and girl, a small stuffed mouse, and a brass candlestick from India, Mel spread out her books. Granny sat half-watching her and a documentary on the African Rift Valley, sucking boiled sweets noisily, her tired feet, wrapped in pink bedsocks, raised onto a great squashy pouffe made from faded leather with camels painted on to it.

Mel felt her panic subside. It was warm and secure here. Granny wouldn't nag her. She couldn't binge with someone else in the room and she might even get some work done on her English essay. She'd won the battle. The overwhelming desire to ram food into her empty self had been defeated. Mel felt relatively peaceful as she read her notes. It was all going to work out fine.

~ 5 ~

Thursday started off well. Mel was so pleased that the extra kilo had disappeared when she had weighed herself and that she had resisted the temptation to binge, that she read a passage out of her Bible, the psalm about God being a good shepherd, and genuinely thanked him for her victory. Today was going to be great, well, at least an okay sort of day.

But, as usual, Mel was disappointed.

'Mel, I'm not sure which planet you were on when you did this work,' Mrs Graff, the Geography teacher handed her back a project on Land Use Choices in Grizedale Forest. 'The content and ideas are fine, but your spelling and mapwork, well, they are not like you at all.'

'Sorry, Miss.' Mel was increasingly confused about who the 'you' was that she was supposed to be.

'So, re-do some mapwork and correct the spellings.'

'Yes, Miss.' Mel felt so stupid. She never made these sort of mistakes. To make matters worse Mrs Graff was a

31

friend of Mum's and went to their church. Mel felt awkward around her, not sure whether she was a pupil, friend's daughter or fellow Christian, and now she looked a real idiot.

Technology, or CDT, was even worse. They were all making soil moisture meters. Why, Mel wasn't sure, when they could have popped to the shops and bought packets of them, neat strips that changed colour. The meters had to light up if the soil was too dry. Mel found the circuits, wiring, batteries and light bulbs just too much, let alone designing a casing. So did everyone else. The difference was that Mel got into an increasing panic, while the others thought it was a laugh.

'What size plant is that for?' asked Ian, pointing to the wood Mel was painfully shaping as a mould for the plastic casing. 'Looks a bit big.'

'So's yours.'

'But yours would fit a fir tree.'

Sarah joined in. 'Stand it in a pot, Mel, and it'll be bigger than the plant.'

'Hey, your one's bent,' said Liz to Sarah. 'Like a piece of modern art.'

'You could paint it, stick it on a board and call it, call it ...' began Tina.

'Impressions of a soil moisture meter,' Sarah finished.

'Hardly a snappy title.' Sarah turned to Mel. 'You're quiet.'

'It's this mould. I'm on the vacuum former next. It'll never work.'

'Have another go, then. Honestly, Mel, you worry too much.'

Mel felt cross. Why had she ever chosen Technology? Probably because Caroline hadn't studied it? With good reason too, thought Mel. See, you couldn't even make decent GCSE choices.

She had got air bubbles in the vacuum former and the resulting green plastic casing looked like a deformed, warty toad with monstrous boils stretching its surface.

'Chuck it in the re-cycling bin,' Mr Blundell was resignedly kind. 'We'll have another go.'

'Alien being in orbit.' Ian threw the toad across the room into the bin. 'Goal!'

'I'll "goal" you, if you muck about,' said Mr Blundell. Teaching Technology to a load of ham-fisted year elevens would send him into an early grave.

Mel's next two attempts were even worse. By now she had an audience, which didn't help, so Mr Blundell abandoned hope.

'Try again next week, Melanie. Come on, Ian, your turn.'

Ian's worked first time. Mel pretended to join in the laughter but inside she felt like crying. She was so hungry, she had got to eat. Mum hadn't seen that she had fed her breakfast to Benjy, while trying to remember the French for going to the shops. She'd have to eat her lunch, but even after lunch break the gnawing pain inside her wouldn't stop. By the evening Mel knew she had got to rush into the arms of a pile of food soon, or she was scared what might happen. Scared that she would go raving mad, that she would break down in class.

The decision was made. Tomorrow night, just over twenty-four hours away, she'd find a safe place and satisfy the growing craving, but tonight she just had to survive. Mum was baking so she couldn't get into the kitchen and her secret store of chocolate was used up. It had better be Granny's room again.

Granny was at a missionary meeting listening to someone talk on relief work in Rwanda. The more depressing the stories, the more she enjoyed the evening. Mel went into her living-room and curled up on a sagging horsehair sofa to watch television and plot what she could eat tomorrow.

In the distance the phone rang. Mel ignored it and a few minutes later her Mum burst into the room, red-faced from cooking, and out of breath.

'What are you doing in here?' She didn't wait for an answer. 'That call was for you.'

'Who was it?'

'Sarah. Seven-forty tomorrow night outside the Cineplex, that new film you wanted to see.'

'I don't now, not tomorrow.'

Mum looked irritated. 'I told her yes. Good grief, Melanie, you've talked enough about it. She's booking the tickets, so you'll have to go.'

'Thanks, Mum.' The attempt at sarcasm was lost on her. How dare she make arrangements for me, making my decisions, acting like she's God. Mel thumped the sofa in anger. I'm fed-up, sick to death of being treated like a kid one minute and like the immaculate Caroline the next. And I haven't got the money, well not enough for the cinema and food. Why the heck does she have to interfere? Can't the woman get a life of her own?

Meanwhile the woman in question was blissfully unaware of her younger daughter's reaction, as she made muffins, temporarily forgetting her diet, and read her Psychology textbook. Mel hunted round her Granny's room. You'd think in all that clutter there would be the odd ten or fifty pence piece. But, oh no, all Granny's change would be in her fat clasp purse, further secured by an elastic band, in the bottom of her huge calico shoulder bag, with *Fun-filled Florida* stamped all over it.

There was no money anywhere, not even by Dad's

side of the bed, or dropped on the floor, nor in Mel's ancient piggy bank, nor by the telephone. Even Mum's bag was down in the kitchen watched over by the nosey hawk. Mel felt like a criminal, thinking horrid thoughts about Mum, plotting to steal odd coins. Well, it was Mum's fault anyway, for saying she would go to the cinema.

Mel suddenly remembered. The non-dairy food fad. Letting herself quietly out of the house by the front door, she crept round the back to the dustbin. Buried beneath vegetable peelings, egg-shells and used tissues she found her treasure. A packet of butter and a wrapped slab of hard cheese. What a relief! She'd got something at last. Mel secreted them in her room and forced herself not to start now.

Friday passed slowly but Mel didn't mind. After Mum had left for work and before Dad had come home, Mel had helped herself to a packet of Weetabix from the back of the cupboard. No one except Caroline ate them, and they were left over from her Christmas visit. Seventeen of them, Mel counted.

Whatever happened today didn't matter. The stores were in. Okay, so it wasn't as exciting as Monday night, no gateau, no ice cream, but it was the best she could do. All thoughts of resisting the urge to binge had gone, flown away. The lion was waking up and wouldn't go back to sleep again properly until it had been satisfied.

Sarah wittered on about the film all day long and Mel knew she would have to wait until after the cinema to let herself free.

'They were nearly sold out, it being the first week,' said Sarah. 'Tina's coming as well. Liz is off with the fabulous Pete.' Sarah rolled her eyes heavenwards. 'It'd be funny if they were at the film as well. We could watch them.'

'Rather you than me,' said Mel. Liz and Pete got on her nerves.

At last the film started and for a brief two hours Mel was almost able to lose herself in another world. A world where the heroine was beautiful, the hero a breathtaking hunk, where misunderstandings which threatened all were resolved, and where, in the end, the two of them, the two beautiful people, rode off into the sunset together. If only! thought Mel. If only it was like this, and I was the girl, and the sun shone, and I could wander over vast prairie lands with my gorgeous lover. If only.

Cold reality drenched her, like icy water from a bucket, as they left the warm, snug haven of the cinema and caught the bus home.

'Do you want to come in for a bit?' asked Sarah.

'No, I said I'd be back.' The lion's roar was ferocious. Running home, Mel stumbled in the house and forced herself to have a normal conversation with Mum. Yes, the film was ace. Yes, he was gorgeous, and, finally, yes, she was tired but she was going to have a bath.

With great expectation Mel grabbed her goodies from her room and, locking the door, ran the bath. The butter had softened near her radiator, so she dipped the Weetabix in it, alternating great bites of the dripping cereal with chunks of cheese. She ignored the fact that the cheese had a distinct greenish tinge round the edges and pushed as much as she could into her gaping hole deep within. Melted butter softly splattered on the tiled floor and she scooped the congealing globules up with her fingers, until nothing was left, and even the wrappers had been licked clean.

Mel had forgotten the water and container, so scooped handfuls of cold liquid out of the sink. She had remembered to turn her portable radio on loud to mask the ghastly retching sounds. It was harder than last time, the food was more solid and after three sessions Mel had to accept that no more Weetabix would return. Frantically she ate a half a bar of chocolate laxative from out of the bathroom cupboard. That should deal with any food that had got into her system.

'Mel, are you going to be long?' It was Mum. 'I want a shower.'

'Ten minutes.' Hurriedly Mel went through the disinfectant routine, leapt into the tepid bath, splashed bubble bath everywhere and opened the window to let in gusts of untainted fresh air. Frantically she scrubbed her teeth, squeezing the toothpaste straight onto them in an effort to cover over the smell of vomit.

It hadn't been so good. It was too rushed. The full, safe, comfortable feeling had hardly lasted any time at all, and the fear of discovery had marred her special time. Repulsed at the events of the last twenty-five minutes, Mel wrapped herself in a towel and threw the Weetabix, cheese and butter wrappers out of the window as Mum banged on the door. It was all out of control. She was out of control and the hungry lion was only partially content.

~ 6 ~

Mel liked to have a lie-in most Saturdays before doing something with her friends, but gripping stomach ache had her up and in the bathroom before eight. At least the laxatives were working, but the stabbing pain was horrendous as Mel's body tried to cope with ten times the normal dose. But it was worth it. That cheese must have been so fattening and now there could not be much of it left. The scales reassured her. Half a kilo down!

Staggering downstairs for a mug of tea, Mel found Mum up, taking notes from her already well-highlighted text book. She was wearing a thick red velour dressing gown and her hair was in rollers. Mel thought Mum could have mastered the art of blow-drying by now, instead of looking like a surprised hedgehog.

'I thought I'd cook Dad a fried breakfast,' said Mum. 'He's off this weekend.'

'To Chipping Sodbury?'

'Well, yes, but I meant he is off work. He'll go family tree hunting after he's had a sleep. What are you doing today, Mel?'

'Not sure.'

'Shall we do some French?'

'Just weekdays, eh, Mum. Anyway, you've got your assignment to do and I've some Geography.'

'What?'

'Oh, just maps, but they take ages.' Mum would go off at the deep end, if she saw the, as yet, uncorrected project.

Mum rummaged through the cupboards, getting Dad's food ready.

'Mel, have you seen the Weetabix?'

'No.'

'I just fancied one. I'm sure there was a box here.'

'Perhaps Caroline took them back. She likes them.'

'Caro? Don't be silly. Her college is catered for. I don't understand it. And another thing I don't understand is what has happened to the bin.'

'Bin?'

'When I let Benjy out there was rubbish blown everywhere and even a butter wrapper stuck on the drainpipe, quite high up. In fact I think I saw a Weetabix carton then, but I'm sure I didn't throw it away.'

'How strange,' said Mel. 'Perhaps it was a fox.'

Help, she'd forgotten to put the lid on the dustbin, and forgotten about throwing the food packaging out of the bedroom window. She would have to be more careful. Mum would get suspicious. Somehow Mel had got to find a way of getting food without pinching it from the kitchen.

A sudden stab of pain sent her running from the kitchen to the bathroom. This was appalling, she felt totally drained.

'Mel, are you all right?' Mum was outside the door.

'I've got a bit of a tummy upset. I'll be fine.'

'It must have been something you ate.'

How true! thought Mel. 'Yes, I suppose so.'

Mum insisted on giving her protesting body a dose of kaolin and morph to stop the runs. Mel felt like a chemical experiment was going on inside her as the laxatives vied with the medicine. All morning long her stomach churned until it felt as if it would explode and Mum kept on making her drink lots of liquids. Mel could feel the drinks sloshing around inside her. She lay on the bed, doing map work on her lap. She was convinced she could see her abdomen moving by itself as gassy bubbles pummelled her battered innards. Grabbing her ever available tape measure, Mel checked herself. The F T Index was up two centimetres. The Fat Tum Index showed the binge-purge hadn't been successful even though the scales still registered the half a kilo loss. Repulsed at the churning mass, Mel snuggled under the duvet, still Caroline's, and wished she could sleep the day away.

At one o'clock Sarah arrived and, reluctant to disturb the pristine tidiness of the house, she insisted they went out. As they couldn't think of anything else to do, and were both broke, they took Benjy to the park. Mel wished she was a dog. She could sleep, play, eat or walk and do just what she wanted. Benjy didn't have to think about anything. He just lived for the moment and accepted whatever life offered him. Look at him now, lost in the rapture of digging through a pile of well-rotted beech leaves.

By the time the two girls had discussed every scene from the film and had had a friendly argument about whether or not the hero should have told his own true love about his undying devotion much earlier in the story, the dog was filthy and Sarah was starving.

'I can't take Benjy back like this,' said Mel.

'Come to my house. He can play in the garden and dry off. The smell of the pond will wear off eventually.'

'You sure?'

'Course. We can always hose him down if it doesn't. Anyway I've got to do toasted sandwiches for our Kevin and Jack. Mum's out.'

It didn't take much to persuade Mel. If she kept with other people, kept busy, it would stop her feeling so dreadful about herself.

A familiar pain gripped her. Oh, no, not here in the park. Not those terrible toilets. She bent double, distress etched across her face.

'What's the matter?' Sarah was all genuine concern.

'Stomach ache.'

'Oh, bundle of funs.'

'You what?'

'The runs.'

'I've got to get to the loo.' Mel staggered across to the dilapidated pavilion and changing rooms. The toilets were locked but someone had broken down part of the door in the Gents'. While Sarah stood guard, Mel sobbed as she used the cracked toilet in the stench-filled, graffiti covered cubicle. She felt nothing but revulsion, at this place, at what she had done to herself. A few months ago she wouldn't have been seen dead in a place like this. Now her fragile self-respect had crumbled completely. It had come to this, cramped over a filthy loo, and all by her own choice.

'You look terrible,' Sarah stated the obvious as Mel came out. 'Let's get home. What's the matter? You were fine at the cinema.'

'Must have been something I had for supper.' Mel

could never tell anyone she'd eaten seventeen weetabix, a packet of butter and nearly a kilo of cheese, let alone the chocolate laxative.

'I'd cut out suppers, if I was you,' Sarah joked. 'They don't seem to agree with you.'

Who or what does, thought Mel.

'You know, Mel, we've known each other for ages.'

'Yes, why?'

'Well, if something was wrong, you'd tell me, wouldn't you?'

'Course,' Mel lied.

'Well, is there? Anything wrong?'

For a brief moment Mel longed to tell her friend everything, but she couldn't. No way could she stand the look of loathing and repugnance that would gallop over Sarah's face.

'No, course not.'

Sarah was not deterred. 'Me and Liz and Tina, we think, you're, well different.'

'Different?'

'Not like you used to be. Quieter, off on your own. You were always the life and soul of the party, a real good laugh, messing around, telling jokes. I don't mean to sound nasty, but you're not fun any more.'

Mel felt tears spring unwanted into her eyes and forced herself not to cry.

'So that's why we wondered if something was up,' Sarah persisted.

'I told you, no. Just a stomach upset.'

'It's just that if you get much quieter, like at school, we'll turn round and you won't even be there.' In the silence that followed, Mel's thoughts ran free. 'Wouldn't even be there!' Well, it wouldn't matter if she wasn't, would it? No one would miss me. I'm no fun. I'm too quiet, a flipping drag to be with. Even my friends don't like me. They'll guess, they've already got their suspicions. And Mum? I'm nothing but a disappointment to her. And Dad? He's too wrapped up in work and blasted family trees to notice. He's got a better relationship with his long-dead ancestors than with me. And Caroline, call me Caro now please. What about Caro?

Mel wasn't sure what she thought about Caro. She's clever and fun and got lots of friends and looks great, but, said another little voice, that's not her fault. She's not all these things to spite you. It isn't her fault that she's like she is, and, added the voice, you're like you are. I can almost make two lists. Caroline equals clever, nice, popular, attractive and me, I equal average, boring, lonely and ugly. It's just not fair.

'So, what do you think, Mel?'

'Eh?' Mel hadn't heard a word Sarah had said.

' Oh, forget it, you're hopeless. Here, take Benjy round the back. Do you want a toasted sandwich?'

'No, thanks.' Hopeless, that about summed her up.

'I'll open you a tin of soup, then.' Sarah was used to caring for others. 'Watch that bike.' But it was too late. Mel had tripped over the motor-bike that was half in and half out of the back door, and sent it crashing in the door frame. Darts of wood splintered off and a jagged scratch mark scarred the length of the back door.

'I'm so sorry, really sorry.' Mel began but Sarah and Kevin were laughing. 'The door, I'll pay.'

'Don't be so daft.' Kevin, smelling of oil, heaved her up. 'No one will notice another mark. You've got grease all over your jeans.'

'Mum'll kill me.' Mel had said it before she could stop herself.

'No worries. Borrow a pair of Sarah's and I'll chuck

these in the wash after I've had a go at them with my magic goo.' Kevin could be quite nice-looking, under the wild curly hair and oil-smeared face, thought Mel with surprise. 'I'm a dab hand at grease removal. My special subject, I call it.'

'Only one you've got,' said Sarah. Her brother had been unemployed since he left school three years ago. No one in the Phipps' residence seemed to mind, and he spent his time doing up motorbikes and re-selling them. It was rumoured that Kevin was going to college to study to be a mechanic but no one had actually seen him there.

For a glorious moment Mel toyed with the image that flashed on her brain. She could just see Mum's face if she took Kevin home and announced he was her boyfriend. She giggled to herself, not that she fancied Kevin, he was more like a big brother, but Mum's reaction would be unforgettable.

'Hey, it laughs,' Kevin said to Sarah. 'The friend laugheth!' And the three of them started to laugh, not sure what about, while the toasted cheese and onion sandwiches slowly burnt under the grill.

~ 7 ~

Next day was Sunday and Mel was in a good mood, for her. She'd stayed at Sarah's until late and enjoyed playing with Jack her little brother, and being teased by Kevin. She decided she would go to church with Granny.

Granny was ready and waiting far too early. Her grey curls were hidden under a brown felt pancake that had started life as a hat. She was wearing a maroon woollen coat that was too big but had been a half-price bargain in the January sales eight years ago. The ensemble was completed by fur-lined leather boots with bits of fur poking out of the top, as if a small mammal had got trapped inside them. As it was Sunday, the calico bag had been exchanged for a vast blue leather hold-all which contained Granny's essentials for life, keys, hairbrush, change of underwear because 'you never knew' (what, Mel hated to think), a novel to pass on to a friend, a small photo album with all the grandchildren as toothless babies, a bag of boiled sweets, stuck together, and a Bible that would not have looked out of place on a large pulpit.

It was the old familiar story of Jesus feeding the five thousand with five loaves and two fish. Mel didn't listen while the vicar made a series of points based on the story. If only God could do that with my food, it would solve the problem, she thought. I could get an iced bun, break it up and it would last for ever. I don't like fish, though, so I'll not bother with that. The vision of multiplying tins of tuna invading her room made her grin.

However it wasn't funny. Everywhere I go I think about food. Food, nothing else. Even here at church, I just can't get away from it.

Someone was saying the prayers. The voice asking God to help the starving millions, was familiar. Mel came out of her daydream. It was Mrs Graff, the Geography teacher, who Mel suspected had been unsuccessfully trying to get Mum interested in Christianity for years. Mel wished she didn't do things up at the front; it was so public. Everyone knew Mrs Graff was a Christian, what with her running the school Christian Union, that Mel avoided, and organising events at church.

Mel had no problem in believing in God, in the facts of the gospel, in salvation. It just wasn't something she wanted to talk about. It was private, like a room in her life that she kept locked and wandered into when she felt the need. It felt odd to talk to God about the food problem. After all, here he was feeding thousands who were hungry, while she gorged and puked. He would be as disgusted and appalled with her as anyone, if he knew.

But he does, said an annoying voice deep inside. He knows everything, all about you. Mel smothered the voice. It didn't bear thinking about. It was too dangerous to even think about all the food she wasted when so many hadn't enough to eat.

At lunch, a traditional roast with all the trimmings,

Mel decided to tell her parents what she wanted. She had to resolve the financial difficulties somehow.

'Dad,' she began, tackling the easier of the two. 'I'm nearly sixteen, so is it all right if I look round for a Saturday job?'

'Sounds okay.' Dad was eager to get back to his ancestral charts after an enthralling few hours in Chipping Sodbury yesterday. 'In a shop or something?'

'Yes, or maybe, if I can't get Saturdays, I'll do a couple of evenings.'

'You'll do no such thing!' Mum served stewed fruit into sloshy pools on the best china.

'But, Mum, Dad said ...'

'Dad hasn't thought. Honestly, Andrew, use your brain. She's got exams!'

'You make it sound like a terminal disease!' said Dad, trying to lighten the atmosphere.

'And,' said Mum, ignoring him, 'with those grades she needs to work hard, not waste time in some shop or other.'

'But Mum ...'

'I don't know what's up with you, Melanie. You don't need to work. You have your allowance, every month. What's wrong with that?'

'It's not enough.'

'Not enough!' Mum was getting irate. 'You hardly ever go out.'

'The cinema, last Friday.'

'You don't buy clothes,' Mum ignored her interruption. 'What do you do with it?'

Mel avoided answering, as Granny came valiantly to her rescue. 'You're too hard on Melanie, Janet. I think it would do her a power of good to get a little job, be that bit independent, see what the real world is like.'

Mum's anger was re-directed to her own mother.

'Oh,' you would, would you? Work was always the most important to you, wasn't it?'

'The money was,' said Granny amicably. 'Let Melanie do what she wants and be independent.'

'Independent! She doesn't need to be independent.'

If I creep away now, thought Mel, they won't even notice I've gone. Why does Mum always think she knows best? Granny hasn't a hope against her. She thought of magazine articles she had read about reasoned family discussions, where everyone had their say, and was listened to. It's all lies, she thought, no one listens to me. Never.

But Dad had tried. As Mum and Granny continued their verbal sparring he leaned across the table. 'Tell you what, Mel, drop the job idea for a while and I'll increase your allowance by a pound a week. Okay?'

Mel resigned herself. 'Okay, Dad, thanks.' No job and a measly extra pound. What use is that? Four Mars bars, three cheap white loaves or Danish pastries. It's not enough, I can't manage like that.

Mum eventually calmed down. Like a spitting cat she had won her verbal fight with Granny. How she had ever come to live with them, Mel couldn't remember. She'd always been there in her little flat. Mel wondered if Granny actually enjoyed these noisy encounters. She looked quite flushed and energised by the battle. Mum was victorious, Dad was washing up tunelessly humming 'Onward Christian Soldiers' and Mel, well, she knew there was no point in her wanting anything.

After a boring afternoon staring at Maths and punctuated only by a phone call from Caroline – the Doctorate funding had been confirmed, oh, joy! – Mel went to the evening service with Dad. They walked in unison along the dark streets.

'Twice in one day, Mel,' he joked. 'Bit much for you?'

'I'll see Tina and maybe Sarah.'

'And maybe some of the lads. Daniel is it?'

'Mark,' Mel could have bit her tongue. Talking with Dad about lads was off-limits, so she changed the subject and listened to the excruciatingly boring detail of what the parish records were like at Chipping Sodbury and exactly how long Granny had insisted on staying at the café on the way back.

It is odd, thought Mel, sitting in the crowded church. Here I am surrounded by all these people, squashed between Tina and Sarah, yet I'm so alone. No one knows who I am or what I am like. I'm just Melanie Chambers, who is to go to university, whose sister is at Oxford. They don't know, and they don't care, not even Dad over there. I wish he didn't sing so loudly. I can hear him from six rows away.

Mel had only come to church for her second visit that day to get away from home, from thinking, from tantalising images of food-laden tables, groaning platters of fresh cream cakes, mountains of chocolates. It had not worked. Even here, in God's house, while she sang about the glorious Creator, or bowed her head in a pretence of prayer, the visions threatened to engulf her.

She tried counting the bricks on the front wall, bending a finger each time she reached a century. The huge carved words *Jesus is Lord*, which stretched the width of the wall, seemed to be jumping out at her. So, Jesus is Lord, she'd said it, heard it, read it, millions of times, but what did it mean? What did it have to do with Melanie Chambers, who was fast becoming very weird. Not a lot, she thought, as the service ended.

'Are you coming for coffee?' asked Tina. 'She's invited all the young people back.'

Why not? Anything was better than going home now. She couldn't binge if she was with people. She couldn't binge with no food anyway, so coffee was the only option.

'I don't know.'

'Oh, go on,' Tina grinned. 'You always used to.'

Mel looked at her. What had Sarah said yesterday? Something about them talking and her not being fun any more. Well, if being fun meant going to someone's house for coffee, then she'd do it, even if she hated every minute of it.'

'Okay. Where are we off to?'

'Mrs Graff's. She's cool, for an oldie.'

Mrs Graff's! Why hadn't she asked where they were going before she said yes? It was too late now.

Mel felt awkward in the big cream and brown living-room, even though she had been there, often with Mum, loads of times before.

'Hello, Melanie. It's nice to see you.' Mrs Graff sat down next to her and ignored the coffee that sloshed over the brim of Mel's mug and splattered the cream sofa with polka dots. Mel started to get up to clean it. 'No problem, I'll do it later. We've not seen you at After-Eights for weeks.'

'After-Eights!' Even the name of the Sunday evening coffee times made Mel long for the dark bitter chocolate with soft white mint inside.

Mrs Graff continued, 'So have you been busy?'

'Yes, Miss, work and that, you know.'

'Melanie, you don't need to call me Miss here, you know. Vicki does fine. So you've lots of work on?'

'Yes.' No way could Mel call her Vicki. 'The exams, projects, all the usual stuff.'

Vicki Graff turned to look straight at her. 'I've been thinking about you quite a bit lately ...' Not another one, thought Mel. 'I might be wrong, but it struck me you might be working too hard, studying too much.' She paused. 'I know I told you to rework your Geography project, but you've got nothing to worry about. You're doing fine.'

Mel didn't know what to say. Fine, Mrs Graff thought she was doing fine. Pity her friend Janet Chambers didn't. In fact, Vicki Graff was treating her like a human being.

'Anyway, Mel, take it from me, we're all pleased with how you are doing, just don't take it too seriously. Here, have a biscuit. Could you pass them round for me?' She moved off to welcome a couple of new girls.

Mel passed the tempting biscuits around the room. On the one hand it was good, because it gave her chance to at least say hello to everyone, including Mark who was even more gorgeous close up. The sad, lonely feeling crept away as Mel acted out her 'nice, fun girl at the party' routine.

On the other hand, circulating with the biscuits was appalling. The glossy chocolate fingers piled carelessly next to the jammy dodgers and iced gems screamed 'Eat me!' at her, while the bourbons, digestives and coconut rings called, 'Go on, no one will notice!

They would though, if Mel did what she really wanted to, if she buried her face into the sweet delights in front of her, people would notice all right. They would despise and hate her. She had to get away.

Mel made herself say a calm goodnight to Tina and Mrs Graff and carefully let herself out of the house. Like an Olympic sprinter she ran home, only slowing down to steady her racing heart and to catch her wheezing breath. Forcing herself to walk normally, Mel knew this could not go on. It was getting worse. She was obsessed. She was going mad.

~ 8 ~

The next week started badly and got worse. Those studying Geography were off on a long weekend field trip to North Wales. When it had first been mentioned, a year ago, Mel had looked forward to it. A few days messing around in rain-soaked hills, covered in mud, looking at glacial features in their landscape, with her friends. They'd have some great laughs, even though late January was a dumb time to go away. Now, though, everything had changed.

'What if I need to binge?' said Mel to Benjy, who at least gave her his rapt attention when she talked to him. 'I can't go away, not four days and three nights. I'll never manage. Even if I eat on Thursday night, I might not last out until I get home again. I've just got to get out of it, be ill or something.' Benjy looked at her as if he understood and put his paw on her knee.

'Or, of course, I could just stop it. I could, you know, Benjy. See, last night I didn't even eat one of the biscuits, and I didn't touch one. Okay, so I wanted to, but I didn't.

I could stop it. It won't be hard. After all, I only need to choose not to take food and put it in my mouth.'

Mel refused to think about the demanding, aggressive, roaring lion within. It was asleep at the moment. It did not exist. 'So, Benjy, I'll stop over-eating, and I'll try to get out of the field trip. That way I'll hedge my bets. I'll be fine, you see.'

However, Mel was deluding herself. Trying to get out of the field trip was a nightmare. She could handle Mrs Graff and school if only she could get a letter from Mum or Dad saying that she could not go. But for what reason? She could fake an illness, one that did not mean going to the doctor, but did mean staying at home. She would try a headache. Mel need not have bothered.

'Perhaps you need glasses,' said Mum when Mel told her she had a headache that evening. 'I'll make you an optician's appointment.'

'Or it could be your teeth,' said Granny.

'Teeth! Mother, don't be silly.'

'If you clench your teeth a lot, you can get headaches,' Granny was adamant. 'I read it in a magazine.'

'If you clench yours, they'll drop out, Mother. Anyway, Mel doesn't do anything with her teeth.'

'Except clean them.' Granny was going to have the last word.

'Or it might be tension in your neck. Here, sit still, Mel. I'll massage it.'

Mel quite enjoyed Mum's massage while the amateur doctors' discussion continued.

'It could be a brain tumour and I'll be dead in days,' said Mel, but no one listened. The headache was a stupid idea, anyway, it was hardly going to last a week!

Plan B had to be plotted, so Tuesday found Mel attempting to put that into action. She waited until

Mum was relaxed and got her talking about how well her Psychology assignment was going. Mel knew Mum's weakness, education. She would try to exploit it.

'Mum, you know this field trip?'

'Friday, that reminds me, have you waxed your boots?'

'Not yet. Mum, I don't think it is a sensible idea to go.' Mel hoped Mum would rise to the 'sensible' bait. She did.

'Sensible? Why?'

Mel launched into her prepared speech. 'Well, I'm doing okay at Geography, but I really need to put a lot of effort into CDT, Music and French, and I'd quite like an 'A' in Maths. So it doesn't seem sensible to go away for a few days to concentrate on one of my best subjects and not to be able to do any work on the others. It doesn't make logical sense to me.' Logic was another of Mum's friends.

Mum was thoughtful. It was working!

'You've thought this all out, haven't you, Melanie?'

'Yes, Mum.'

'I can see it makes common-sense.' Mel was winning! 'It's a shame to concentrate on one subject. You couldn't study any others while you're there?'

'No, Mum, I've seen the timetable. We're far too busy.' Mel didn't mention the dark evening hours of free time.

'I see.' A silence. Victory was in sight! She wouldn't have to go! 'I can understand what you're saying, Mel, and I'm very pleased you're taking your studies serious-ly.' Great, thought Mel, I'm in her good books as well. 'The field trip is essential, and paid for, I'm afraid.' Mel's high hopes were shot down in flames. 'Of course you'll have to go. If you work hard, cut down on TV, you've plenty of time for the other subjects.'

'But, Mum ...'

'So I appreciate your concern, but you are going. You

said you were looking forward to it.'

'I was, but ...'

'I'll get Dad to go up the loft and get your big ruck-sack down.'

'I'll do it.' Mel was resigned to her fate. Plan B had failed. 'There's a couple of other things up there I want.'

It was no use fighting it. Mel felt gutted. For a few minutes she thought Mum had listened and understood, but she was fooling herself. An empty ache started to grow inside her, insisting it was filled. Mel went into the kitchen and grabbed a loaf of bread that was defrosting. Running upstairs, she pulled the loft ladder down and climbed up into the cold dark attic. The dim light bulb sent cavernous shadows across the space.

Quickly finding her big rucksack and sleeping bag, Mel curled herself into a small bundle. Ripping open the loaf wrapper, she forced the hard bread into her mouth, chewing at the tasteless white mess, until at last she had enough saliva to swallow the thick stodge. No drink! She forced every slice down, as if ramming soil into an empty plantpot, filling up the gaps deep inside her, burying the feelings she could neither identify nor cope with.

Mel felt dreadfully sick and just made it down the cold aluminium loft ladder to the bathroom in time. In her haste she forgot her radio or to turn on the shower to cover the sounds of her retching. The creamy mass had to be regurgitated, no matter what.

'Mel, is that you?' It was Granny, off to the mid-week Bible study at church. 'Are you ill?'

'Just messing around, Granny. Making funny noises.' She started to sing.

'Well, it's nice to hear you playing for once. You know what they say, "All work and no play makes Jack a dull lad".'

What was she on about? 'Have a nice meeting, Granny,'

sang Mel, warbling her voice. Granny would think she was barmy but better that than thinking the truth. After cleaning her teeth, Mel climbed back up the loft, got her stuff, came down, lay on her bed and tried to think about the effects of the Irish potato famine on American Immigration, until she fell asleep.

Mel woke early on Wednesday morning still wearing her crushed school uniform. As she showered she talked to herself.

'So, the field trip is on. You can't get out of it. You'll just have to stop the food thing. I know, pray and read your Bible and see if that helps. It won't do any harm.'

And that's what Mel did. In all her spare moments she read her Bible, even at lunch break with it well hidden behind a paperback. Starting at Genesis, she whizzed through creation, got caught up with Noah and his ark, wandered around the Near East with Abraham and decided she was glad she had not been alive in Joseph's time.

She gamely ploughed through the plagues in Egypt, the Exodus and the Israelites interminable to-ings and fro-ings in some barren wilderness, as they strove to reach the Promised Land. This was more than Mel had. She stared at her ceiling, after school on Thursday, and thought about it.

What would her promised land be like? It wouldn't be very helpful if it was flowing with milk and honey, like the one in the Bible. No, my land would look pretty much the same as around here, but the people would be different, well, perhaps not Granny, or Mark at church. Everyone else would be, though. I'd be different.

Mum would loosen up and enjoy life. Dad wouldn't have to work so hard and he could find another hobby. Anything – fishing, golf, even train-spotting. Caroline could get spots or greasy hair, something to spoil her perfection and maybe she could fail at least one thing. She even passed her driving test first time.

And me, what would I be like? It's hard to know. Thinner, prettier, cleverer, yes, I suppose I would be all those things, but would I be happier? Not unless I could be different inside. In my promised land I would only think about food at meal times. I would be listened to. I would be important.

Mel shut her Bible angrily. This was all a waste of time. Old adventure stories had got nothing to do with her. Admittedly God was involved with these different people but they were nothing like her. She could not relate to a childless Abraham, a reluctant leader Moses, a warrior Joshua or the doings of a primitive nomadic tribe. She had read all these chapters, two whole books of the Bible, and all it had done was keep her occupied.

It had not helped. 'God, why don't you do something? It's no use to me that you sent plagues in Egypt, provided food in the desert or helped women get pregnant. Half the time I don't know where you are or what you are doing. Why don't you cancel the field trip, or make me different, or give me a break from being me?'

Mel's religious and theological musings ended abruptly as Mum came into her room, without knocking.

'Reading your Bible? Dad will be impressed!' Mum's voice was edged with sarcasm. 'I thought it was about time you got ready for tomorrow, the field trip, but perhaps I could check you on your French first.'

'Oh, Mum, not now.'

'We've missed a few mornings.' Mum flopped into an easy chair by the bed. 'Where were we, ah, here I think, Past tense of irregular verbs.' Mum was away and Mel struggled through the exercise. She would never be able to stand up to her. Never.

~ 9 ~

Mel packed her rucksack and checked that she had got everything she needed for the field trip. There was at least one good thing about the trip. She would get away from Mum for a bit.

After watching a soap opera with Granny, Mel went back to her room to study. It looked as if it had been burgled. All the contents of her rucksack had been tipped out onto the bed and her mum was sitting in the middle of the chaos, sewing.

'I thought I'd better sew your name into your clothes, Melanie. We don't want any getting lost, do we?'

Mel was speechless. How dare she? How dare she rifle through her bag? And name tapes! She was nearly sixteen not six, for goodness' sake.

'And I thought your old tracksuit would be better than your jeans and I don't know why you've put your new Christmas jumper in. I've swapped it for that thick Arran one of mine. I don't want you to catch cold.'

If only I had the courage to scream at you, thought

58

Mel, push you over into my clothes and throw your flaming sewing box out of the window.

'I've got your wellies out of the shed.' Mum looked pleased with herself.

Wellies! No one in their right mind wore wellies. She would be the laughing stock of year eleven.

'I've put them in this freezer bag, in case they get muddy.' Mum laughed. 'Well, of course they'll get muddy in the countryside in January, so, Melanie, make sure you put them back in the bag when you take them off.'

'Yes,' said Mel, deciding that the best place to hide the offensive wellington boots was in the front garden, under the thick laurel hedge. Old eagle eyes wouldn't spot them there.

'Now, have you got your books?'

'We don't need any. Everything's at the centre,' Mel told her. 'It's got a big equipped study room, you know, with maps and things.'

'Well, I got you this as a treat.' Mum produced a green and pink file with Melanie Chambers in huge letters on it. 'It matches your room.' She digressed. Mel hated the stupid file. The way Mum was looking, you would have thought she had given her a hundred pounds.

You haven't a clue, thought Mel. Wellies, files, Arran jumpers, name tapes, do you want me to look a complete fool? Why don't you just get on and live your own life?

Suddenly Mel realised. That was it. Mum lived out her life through her daughters. It was always 'Caro this' or 'Mel that'. The times she had had to listen in squirming embarrassment as Mum went on about her brilliant family to anyone who had ever listened.

A memory flashed onto the screen of her mind. Mel was only little, about four and it was a really hot day.

Although Caroline was ten, Mum still met her at the school gates. It was before Mum went to work.

As Mel had hopped around, trying to miss the cracks in the paving slabs, her dark hair tied up in bouncing pigtails, she had heard Mum talking in a loud voice. About Caroline, some dancing exam she had got merit in. Glancing up she had seen the other woman's face. She looked totally bored, her eyes watching the playground. She wasn't interested in Mum's stories. And Melanie knew something wasn't right. Unable to put it into words, she felt almost ashamed of her mum, who was oblivious to the reaction of those around her.

Now, years later, she still felt ashamed of the insensitive woman who was prattling on about checking biros, and whether Mel had got enough changes of underwear. Mel felt really guilty for feeling the way she did. She knew Mum loved her and genuinely believed she was acting in Mel's interests. She could even understand that her obsession with getting a good education was because she felt she had not had one. But all the understanding didn't make Mel feel any better. She could imagine Sarah in this situation with *her* mum.

'Get your mitts off my stuff,' Sarah would jokingly screech at her mum. 'And forget wellies. I'll sort my stuff out myself.' She'd hug her mum, and her mum would apologise, and leave Sarah to get on with her life. That's what Mel wanted. At least she thought she did, but actually it felt quite scary. She didn't know what her own life was. Slow feelings of unease started to spread inside her and Mel blocked them out by reciting French verbs.

'That's a good idea,' said Mum, looking pleased. 'There's just room for this.' She slid the French revision book into the re-packed rucksack. 'You can be going over your tenses while you trudge up the mountain sides. Did you wax your boots, like I told you to?'

'I'll do it now.'

'In the garage. Don't make a mess.'

Mel went to Granny's room. She never minded mess, but Mel still spread some newspaper on the dining-room table by the window.

As Mel polished her boots, enjoying the feel of the special wax as she rubbed it deep into the leather, Granny came home from her meeting where she had been knitting blankets for earthquake victims.

'Do you know, Mel?' she began, flopping into her armchair and kicking her shoes out of sight. 'I used to change your mum on that table. And your Aunt Sylvia, and Uncle David and our Michael.'

'Change them?'

'Yes, nappies and all that. She was a dreadful squirmer, rolled off one day but our Janet has always been one to bounce back. She's as thick-skinned as they come.'

Mel couldn't imagine Mum as a girl let alone as a baby. She was sick to death of thinking about her. Why couldn't Mum have been more like Granny?

'I got you some goodies at the shop, for the trip.'

Granny tipped out a bag of assorted chocolate bars. Looking at them Mel felt something snap. Four large bars. She had got to have them. Now. But they weren't enough. Nowhere near enough to shut up the lion scratching at her insides.

'Thanks, Granny.' Mel left the room. She'd had an idea. Excitedly she ran into the kitchen. Mum was part way through a video. She would not notice.

Mel tore open the cupboard doors. What could she take? Mum had never believed that story the other day, when Mel had tried to convince her that, no, she hadn't taken a loaf out of the freezer to defrost. She was still muttering about disappearing Weetabix. No, it had to be something Mum wouldn't miss.

In a large empty margarine tub Mel mixed a huge scoop of flour, two eggs, milk, sugar and cinnamon into a batter. She almost dipped her finger in for one lick, but, no, she could wait. The anticipation was one of the best parts of the experience.

'Just taking Benjy out,' she called.

The protesting dog was dragged past every lamppost and interesting smell on the way to the park as Mel half-ran there. It was dark and cold. The park gates were locked but Mel squeezed through a gap in the thick hedge. Burrowing deep into the bushes she felt no fear at being in this blackened place, alone, at night.

Benjy thought it was great and, free from his lead, bounded through the sludgy undergrowth. Mel stumbled over broken branches, unaware that she had grazed her shin, and she didn't feel a stray bramble tug at her coat, making pin prick holes down the sleeve. Mel only knew that she had to find safety.

At last she found the spot and sat on a fallen tree-trunk, knees tucked under her chin. It was like being in a cave, the bare overhanging branches on one side made her a bit vulnerable, but Mel knew that no one could see her through the thick holly bush and trailing fir tree. Benjy leapt around, smelling the food.

'Get away, Benjy, fetch.' She threw a stick which lodged near the base of a fir tree.

Holding the margarine tub in both hands, like a soup bowl, Mel began to drink the glutinous batter. At each mouthful she felt a wave of pleasure sweep over her. More and more poured down her willing throat. The lion was happy.

The chocolate bars followed. Mel couldn't wait to

chew them properly, so she painfully swallowed the bitten chunks. All gone. Replete, full and content, Mel smiled to herself and stretched out her legs, accidentally kicking the dog who had returned from chasing non-existent rabbits.

It was all gone, the food, the confusion, Mum, field trips, wellies, the lot. She was free!

Her stomach heaved. 'Help, I've got to get rid of it!'

The first surge of vomit spewed out of her with no effort, as her stomach protested at the sudden onslaught. After that Mel repeatedly stuffed her fingers down her throat. In the darkness she couldn't tell if all the chocolate bars had returned. It must all be gone by now.

Mel felt dizzy and sat back on the log. Benjy was eating her vomit. He put his front paws on her knees and started licking her coat. Mel felt down her chest, her fingers tacky with the sticky gunge. She'd been sick all over herself.

'What a mess!' She began to cry and Benjy licked her damp face, his doggy breath smelling of raw egg and sweet chocolate. She cuddled him, holding on to him as he cleaned up every bit of her vomit, until he wriggled, eager to be away from her stranglehold.

Mel could cry no more. Exhausted, loathing herself, she blundered out of the park, Benjy dancing in front of her. The dog deposited a huge steaming pile by the park gates and Mel was too wrapped up in her alarming self-repulsion to notice that she had walked straight into it.

Leaving her caked shoes in the porch, she staggered to bed, too depressed to even weigh and measure herself. Living her own life! What a joke! If this was living, then you could keep it.

~ *10* ~

However much I don't want something to happen, I can't stop it, thought Mel, early the next morning, as she cleaned her filthy shoes. I don't want to go on the field trip, but I've got to. I don't want to be Caroline's sister, but I am. I don't want to binge, but I do. I don't want to be fat and ugly, but I always will be.

Mel's mood had, for once, communicated to Mum, who had tried impatiently to hurry her to get ready.

'Dad will take you in the car. He promised he wouldn't be late back from work,' said Mum, irritably.

'I can walk,' replied Mel.

'Not with that rucksack.'

'But ...'

'You'll be round-shouldered and have arthritis by the time you're thirty.'

Mel gave in. Actually lots of her class had got lifts that morning and Mel was pleased to see that most were even more weighed down than she was. There wasn't a wellington boot in sight and Mel hoped hers would stay hidden in the bush until she returned home.

The field centre was a huge stone house perched under some cliffs that looked as if they would topple down with a gust of wind. Inside it was surprisingly warm and bore the scars of countless visits by teenagers. It doubled as an outdoor pursuits centre, the walls covered with posters of macho men dangling off rocky crags, or lycra-clad girls abseiling. The pictures of white water canoeing made Mel determined never to have a go.

There were twenty-two of them studying Geography under the watchful eyes of Mrs Graff, a student teacher nicknamed Ivan the Terrible, with his flashing black eyes and East European accent, and assorted staff from the centre. Mel had difficulty telling who was who. They were all somewhere in their twenties, wore walking trousers and thick fleeces in dark blue and were annoyingly smiley and happy all the time. In their free time they talked about kernmantle ropes, flexible friends, karabiners and hexcentrics. Mel hadn't got a clue what they were on about.

'I told you before, don't clip the prussik loop into your backline karabiner,' Blue Fleece paused. 'Who are you?'

'Melanie Chambers.'

'You're in Cnicht.'

'Cnicht?'

'The dormitory at the front. It's a mountain. See you after lunch.' Blue Fleece One turned back to Blue Fleece Two. 'Then you can reduce slack by pushing the prussik loop as far down the main rope as you can, undo the two half hitches—' The voice faded as Mel found Cnicht.

Sarah, Liz and six other girls were already unpacking. They had kindly left a bunk for Mel. The middle one of a triple wooden coffin.

'Does anyone prefer this bunk?' said Mel, deliberately being casual.

'Why, what's wrong with it?' said Eleanor, on the one above.

'Oh, nothing, I just thought someone else might want it.'

'Well, they don't,' said Sarah. 'Oh, heck, I've forgotten my boots.'

'You can borrow some,' said Mel. 'There are hundreds here.'

'Trust Melanie to know,' said Eleanor. 'Come on, it's lunch time.'

Mel slowly unpacked, not that there was any space left to put her clothes. 'Trust Melanie to know'. What had Eleanor meant by that? That she was a know-all, a big-head? She had only wanted to be helpful to Sarah. Everything she ever said was misunderstood.

The next forty-eight hours ranged from awful to abysmal. The only good point was the Geography. During daylight hours they were thrust into bumpy minibuses, and through steamed-up windows they exclaimed at the sight of corrie lakes, drumlins, U shaped valleys, effects of soil erosion and the rock face where Blue Fleece One had nearly come to grief. This, however, was better than being outside the minibuses.

It rained the whole time. Admittedly it was sometimes heavy rain, and at other times very heavy rain. The only positive aspect was that the rocks were too wet for their special treat – rock climbing and abseiling. Instead Saturday was given over to the delights of exploring around Snowdon. It would have been up Snowdon but for the poor visibility.

'This is ridiculous,' said Sarah. 'All we'll learn from this is how to get pneumonia and survive.'

'It's not that bad,' said Ian, who seemed to be following Sarah around. 'It's nearly stopped.'

'You try drawing the landscape when your fingers are frozen, your paper is wet, and your felt-tip pen leaks,' said Sarah.

'Okay.' Ian grinned, placed his fingers over Sarah's and guided them into a reasonable representation of the scene in front of them. Sarah looked at him and Mel groaned. Not another one! Not another of her friends about to 'fall in love' or go all moony over a lad. Not another one to rub it in that Mel would never get a boyfriend of her own, not that Sarah would ever say that. She might think it, though.

In the shelter of some disused mine workings, the group listened as Mrs Graff extolled the virtues of the view they would have been able to see if the mist would have cleared for a minute. She had done her homework well.

'We're aiming for Bwlch Moch. The Pyg track skirts the northern side of the Tal-y-Llyn ridge and you can see, well, I hope we can sometime, the spectacular ice-scoured defile of the Llanberis Pass. I particularly want you to notice the way in which the ends of the ridges have been sliced off by a former glacier. Also think about the location of the Youth Hostel at Pen-y-Pass ...'

'Wish I was there,' said Sarah.

'It was originally an inn, founded in 1850 to give shelter to weary travellers.'

'Like us,' said Eleanor. 'Mrs Graff, can we go now?'

'Let's just carry on a little more.' And Blue Fleece Two led the straggling group of thickly waterproofed students reluctantly up the mountain until even she suggested going back to the Centre.

'We've some good videos for you this evening,'

said Blue Fleece One, as an incentive.

'The new James Bond?'

'Better still. After an aerial view of Snowdonia, we've a rock climbing training video and maybe there will be enough time for *Match of the Day* on television. Mind you, the reception is a bit hit and miss.'

Like this, thought Mel. Her feet hurt, she felt like a penguin in her borrowed waterproofs, she was cold, hungry, Sarah was talking with Ian, flirting with him, her hair was drenched and today had got nothing to do with getting a Geography GCSE.

'How are you, Mel?' It was Mrs Graff, who looked very young, with her cold, rain-washed face.

'Fine.'

'Enjoying it?'

'Yes, Miss.' Why couldn't she ever say what she really thought?

'We'll do a low level walk tomorrow, the old railway track near Bedgellert. It's a pity about the weather.'

'Yes, Miss.'

'But at least the waterfalls are full. Look at that one over there. Perfect, from a hanging valley.'

Mel pretended to enthuse about the unseen valley. Even during the evening's bird's eye view of Snowdonia, she sat with a fixed smile on her face while just about everyone else mucked about. Sarah fell asleep, or at least pretended to, very close to Ian, so close her head slumped onto his shoulder, and he didn't move it. Mel smiled. Ian might think Sarah was asleep but Mel knew better.

Four of her classmates played cards, two had disappeared, a couple were writing up notes from today, Eleanor was finishing mapwork, Steve and Brian were comparing their athlete's foot fungus, Mrs Graff had taken her glasses off so she was hardly engrossed in the video, and Ivan the Terrible was trying to work out if there was any way he could escape to the local pub for a few pints. And still the video extolled the virtues of glacial mantles, cwms or corries, troughs and screes as well as detailing the history of the area.

Mel wasn't at all interested in Roman Conquests in 71-78 AD, or what Llwelyn ap Gruffyd got up to in guerrilla warfare near Dolwyddelan or in the construction of Telford's suspension road bridge over the Menai Straits to Angelsey.

All Mel wanted to do was to get away, but she couldn't, so she sat still as the wonders of rock climbing unfolded before her eyes. However, she did refuse politely to practise rope knots, despite the hilarity that followed. Ivan the Terrible looked quite good trussed up like a pork joint.

The next morning there was a vote on what to do. Mel did not want to do any of the options, so put her hand up for them all. In the end they all went down to Bedgellert. David and Eleanor fell off a bridge into the raging Glaslyn river and had to be rescued. Mel was terrified but they seemed to think it was great fun, even if they were freezing, as they were whisked off to be dried and to stay in the warm.

The scenery was beautiful, despite the needle-edged rain and the morning was cut short due to the weather. At least they hadn't had to come back the long way over Cwm Bychan.

Steaming, the group crammed into a tea shop and, having bought drinks, were allowed to eat their packed lunches. Not surprisingly few walkers were out and about and the tea shop owner prefered a room full of wet teenagers to an empty shop.

Something was definitely going on between Sarah and Ian, although she had hotly denied it in the dorm last night. Liz was teaching her table how to do rope knots using her anorak cords. Blue Fleeces were still laughing and joking. Sarah was gazing at Ian, whilst pretending to talk to Mel, Ivan the Terrible had nipped to the closest pub on the pretext of buying a postcard and a lively discussion was going on about what would have happened if David and Eleanor had drowned.

'They should never have balanced on the bridge parapet,' said Mel, forcing herself into the conversation.

'Parapet! You mean rail. Honestly, Melanie Chambers, anyone would think you had swallowed a dictionary,' joked one of the lads.

'They feed them dictionaries at their house,' said Liz, not meaning anything by it. 'A to G for breakfast, H to P for lunch and the rest at tea.'

'Course we do,' said Mel, trying to join in the joke. 'That's why I said parapet, you know, p for parapet, it's lunch time.' No one laughed and Mel felt colder inside than she'd felt outside in the wind and rain. Even when she tried to be fun, she couldn't do it. No one liked her. No one.

~ 11 ~

After a couple of hours spent looking at the grey, windswept coastal features near Criccieth, the group trailed back to the Centre. Last, as usual, in the rush for showers or baths, Mel stripped off her wet clothes and sat on the floor of Cnicht dorm. No way was she squeezing into her coffin bunk bed. She hugged her huge bath towel round her, rocking backwards and forwards, trying to comfort the growing disturbance within.

She couldn't win. When she said what she thought, like talking about parapets, people mocked her and didn't like her. Or if she didn't try hard at school, she got it in the neck from Mum. All the time she was trying to please someone, but they all wanted such different things, and it was all too difficult.

The dozing lion growled and turned over, stretching in its long sleep.

Look at now. I could have easily got the shower before Liz or Sarah, but I let them barge past me. I bet all the hot water will have gone by the time it is my turn. Mel sighed. I'll go on one of those assertiveness courses, learn how to stand up for myself. She continued to rock. Don't be so stupid, can you imagine it, please, Sir, I let others take my place in the shower queue, how pathetic!

The door burst open. 'Hurry up, Mel. High tea, whatever that is, in five minutes.' Sarah, half-dried, pranced across the room. 'Why are you sitting on the floor?'

'It seemed like a good idea,' said Mel.

'You look like a baby, wrapped up in that towel,' added Tina, rubbing her hair. 'Get a move on!'

Tea was wonderful. Thick sandwiches, jam and cream sponge cakes, and a huge pile of sticky buns, the currants winking at Mel, sharing her secret. This was to keep them going until a late cooked supper. Mel drank in the scene greedily. If only she could dive full-length onto the table and cover herself in buns.

'Do you know how many calories there are in one of these?' Eleanor twirled a bun round, with disdain. 'Hundreds. Honestly, this place hasn't heard of healthy eating.' She ate one anyway and passed the plate round. Apart from Sarah, few of the girls took any and the lads were eating sponge cakes, which they had divided between themselves with mathematical precision.

Mel dared eat nothing. If she did she wouldn't stop.

'Mel,' said Mrs Graff. 'Do have something. You've used up a lot of energy today.'

'I'm just thirsty, Miss. I'll have another mug of tea.' The steaming liquid only emphasised the emptiness inside, as the tea sloshed around her stomach.

'I need a couple of volunteers to clear up,' said Mrs Graff, 'and then it's time to write up our notes.'

In the stampede from the room and the corporate

groans, Mel was left behind. A glimmer of light flickered in her forlorn heart. There was a way out of this.

'I'll do it, Miss. I've only a bit to write up, but I need to nip to the loo first.'

'Thanks, Mel. You don't know how good it is to have someone to rely on. Come to the study room afterwards.'

'Yes, Miss.' Mel raced upstairs, not to the loo, but to the deserted dorm. Grabbing her pillowcase, the awful white linen one embroidered with violets, she ran downstairs. Making sure no Blue Fleeces could see from the kitchen hatch, she tipped all the remaining buns into the pillowcase and added the discarded, chewy sandwich crusts. Quickly she hid the bulging sack behind a cupboard and, humming tunelessly, began to clear the table.

'You lot soon got rid of that tea.' Mel jumped as a Blue Fleece appeared at the hatch. 'I was looking forward to a bun myself.'

'They were hungry,' explained Mel.

'I don't know why. Your group are a lazy lot,' joked Blue Fleece. 'And wimps. One gust of wind and they want to be indoors with their mummies.'

'Yes,' said Mel, wanting to get away and hide her stash of buns. But Blue Fleece was in a talkative mood and seemed to be encouraged by Mel's monosyllabic 'yes's to give her the benefit of her life history. This included peaks she had climbed, would climb and an offer of watching a video of the knife-edge Aonach Eagach ridge near Glencoe, that evening.

'You'd better join the others,' she said at last, turning to stack the dishwasher. Seizing the opportunity, Mel pushed the bulging pillowcase up the front of her mum's oversized Arran sweater. She threw it on her bunk. The room was such a mess that no one would ever notice. At last she was safe. If the lion started prowling around she could satisfy it. In fact Mel felt a delight of desire and only by quickly going to the study room could she stop herself falling on the lumpy pillowcase, then and there.

Much later that evening, after work had finished, and a supper of sausage and mash had been demolished, Ivan the Terrible organised a game of *Trivial Pursuit* for those who weren't watching dare-devil climbers on the Aonach Eagach ridge. Eventually he got them into four teams. Mel was with Ian, David, who was sneezing after his dip in the Glaslyn, Sarah and Eleanor in Team B.

Mel used to like games but knew they were fraught with difficulties. If she answered all the questions that she knew, then the others would think she was a Nellie-know-all. If she didn't answer, and a crucial move depended on it, or if she got it wrong, they wouldn't like her either. It was as hard as negotiating the terrifying ridge which still flickered on the video in the corner of the room.

'What is the eve of All Saints' Day?' asked Team A.

'Hallowe'en,' said David. 'That's easy.'

'Correct. Now, what are you on?'

'Blue. Geography,' replied David.

'Well, I bet you don't get this. What two countries are linked by the Brenner Pass?'

Team B sat silent. Mel knew it was Austria and Italy, but she wasn't saying.

'Mrs Graff, do you want to be on our team?' asked David. 'At least that way we would have a chance of winning.'

'It wouldn't be fair, David,' said Mrs Graff, who would have loved to disappear and soak in a deep bubble bath. 'Anyway, Mel should know that one.'

'Austria and Italy,' answered Mel reluctantly.

'What a star! Correct. You lot are winning. Good grief, this next question's a cinch, especially for you Melanie, what with you being a Christian and all that.'

Mel grimaced. She did not like being the centre of attention. Fifteen pairs of eyes watched as Team A asked the crucial question.

'In the Bible, did Cain kill Abel, or Abel kill Cain, in the first murder?'

Mel's mind went blank. She must have heard the story of the two brothers so many times, but she couldn't remember who killed who.

'Come on, Mel,' said Sarah. 'I don't know. I've only just started going to church. You've gone for years.'

'You're part of the God-squad, then?' Ian tickled her.

'Sort of. Not like Melanie. Hurry up, Mel, it's our last cheese depending on this.'

I know, thought Mel, I'm not completely stupid, but which one was it? Cain? Abel? I've got a fifty per cent chance of being right, or wrong.

'For goodness' sake,' said Eleanor to her team mate. 'Just say the right one.'

'Abel,' stuttered Mel.

Team A burst out laughing. 'You dumb wit. Wrong! Its the other one, Cain.'

'Trust you to muck it up,' said Eleanor. 'We were winning.'

'I thought you were all religious. You should have known that,' said Sarah, accusingly.

Mel wanted to scream. She couldn't turn the banter back on herself. She couldn't diffuse the situation, admit she had messed it up, join in the laughs and get on with the game.

Slowly she got up and walked from the room. Sarah started to follow her.

'Leave her alone, she's a big baby.' Eleanor called her back.

Patiently Mel went up to her dorm and, with great deliberation, retrieved her pillowcase. She went into the deserted kitchen and took a litre of milk from the fridge. Out through the front door and back round the side of the house, oblivious of the biting wind and the fact that the rain had stopped, Mel sought shelter. Like a wounded animal she looked for a safe place to lick her wounds. A place where no one could find her, where the lion could be fed.

Behind the huge shed, where equipment was stored, was an old lean-to. It looked ramshackle even in the fitful moonlight. Ignoring the *Keep Out* sign Mel pushed open the wooden door and jumped as it squealed in protest. Through the broken roof slates, pin-pricks of moonlight guided Mel as she headed for the far corner. The floor was damp, littered with old wood shavings and abandoned coils of worn climbing ropes, as well as huge flower pots stored for the winter.

As if in a dream, Mel crouched on an upturned pot, back to the door which was now swinging noisily on its unoiled, loose hinges. Making herself as small as possible she began.

The rejected crusts first, softened in milk. Then the buns. Wonderful, sweet, sticky, satisfying, they had stuck together, squashed in the pillowcase. Mel tore them apart, relishing the feel of them in her cold hands. At last she was in control. The lion was being fed. It was starting to purr in contentment. It wasn't a lion anymore, just a fat pussy cat sleeping happily by a warm fire, at peace. No one could harm her. No one could get to her. She was free, free from whatever it was that everyone else wanted from her, free from pain, from struggle. Mel was safe. She had found her refuge in this leaky shed. Mel allowed herself to wallow, like a hippo in mud, in her peaceful happiness, for just a few more minutes. Then it was time to begin 'The Return Journey', as she was starting to call the familiar purge.

Sticking her fingers down her throat she began to heave. It was hard work. The undigested buns were reluctant to leave their resting place. Again and again she sicked up small quantities, unaware that she was making great retching noises and that tears were pouring down her cheeks. She paused. Nearly done.

It was then that she heard it. Footsteps, and they were coming her way.

~ *12* ~

The footsteps got closer. Soft voices intertwined. Giggles. A silence. Mel vaguely wondered who it was but more importantly whether or not they would discover her. The voices started again.

'So will you go out with me?'

'Course.'

'I've been wanting to get to know you better for ages.'

'I hadn't guessed,' said a girl's voice. 'Not until this field trip.'

'But you've guessed now?'

Another long silence. They must be kissing, thought Mel, recognising the voices as belonging to Sarah and Ian. Well, she'd been right about that, at least. Another of her friends nuts about a lad. Mind you, Ian was okay.

Mel crouched quietly, willing them to go back into the Centre. Her stomach was heaving and any minute now she would be sick. Desperately she tried to stop herself but it was no use.

Her stomach's learned behaviour pattern went into

operation and Mel was unable to stop the dry retching as she vomited up yet more sticky buns. She did not realise that she was sobbing.

'What's that?' said Ian, alarmingly close by.

'What?'

'A sort of noise, in the broken-down shed.'

'You're imagining it,' said Sarah, wanting to get back to the hugs and kisses.

'I expect you are right.' Another silence broken only by the muffled sound of Mel hiccuping.

'Listen, there it is again,' said Ian.

'It's nothing.'

'No, listen!'

Sarah sighed. 'Well, whatever it is, it's none of our business.'

'It might be something trapped, an animal or bird maybe.'

'It can't be. Look, the door is half open. An animal could get out. Come on, Ian, forget it. We'd better go back inside.'

Ian was persistent. 'It might be caught in something. Let's take a look. It won't take a minute.'

'What if it's wild, dangerous?' Sarah had had enough of the dimly lit courtyard.

But it wasn't dangerous or wild. It was just very frightened.

'God, don't let them come in here, don't let them find me. This is awful. I can't stand it. Please, make them go back into the house. Get someone to call them. Do something. Please, I can't be found like this.' Mel was suddenly aware of the tell-tale smell of her sick. She tried to kick a few wood shavings over it, but only succeeded in knocking over a flowerpot, which made a doom-laden hollow noise.

'I told you there's something here,' said Ian, triumphantly swinging open the door. 'I knew it.'

Mel held her breath and made herself as small as possible but all in vain. A shaft of moonlight pierced through the open doorway like an accusing finger pointing at her. It probed to the heart of the pile of vomit, lit up the pillowcase and easily picked out the back of the Arran jumper.

'Who is it? Who's there?' Ian and Sarah stood by the threshold. Sarah gave a sudden gasp. 'Good grief! It's Mel! Her jumper. Mel, what on earth are you doing?'

Mel just cried and shook uncontrollably as a reply.

Sarah did not know what to do so tried the jolly approach. 'I know you don't like your bunk bed, but this is a bit extreme!'

No response.

'So, what are you doing?' Sarah moved across to her and slipped in the remains of the milk trickling out of the plastic bottle. 'Mel, you're ill. Ian, fetch Mrs Graff.'

Mel sat upright. 'No, you mustn't, no.' The desperation in her voice stopped Ian in his tracks.

'Look, Mel, it's all right to be ill, although why you have to choose to do it here, not in the bathroom, is beyond me.'

'I'm not ill.'

'Well, what are you, then?'

Mel was at a loss to think of a reply, one that would satisfy Sarah.

'I said,' repeated Sarah, 'what is the matter?'

'Nothing.'

'Nothing!' Ian broke in. 'I've never seen so much sick in my life, and you've got it all down the front of your jumper.'

'Her mum's jumper. You don't think she'd have bought

80

this herself, do you, Ian?' Sarah was momentarily side-tracked.

'It doesn't matter whose jumper it is. The fact is, it's covered in yuck and Mel's wearing it.'

'I was sick,' said Mel, stating the obvious. She started to cry again. 'I was exploring ...'

'Exploring? Eleven o'clock at night? You don't even like the dark,' said Sarah.

'Well, you and Ian obviously do!' Mel replied with uncustomary spirit. 'I was exploring and felt sick.'

'Fetch Mrs Graff, Ian,' Sarah instructed.

'No!' Mel tried to protest.

'Just do it.' Ian wandered off.

'Look, he's gone. Now, tell me, what on earth is the matter?'

'Nothing.'

'Is it your period?'

'No.'

'Have you strained a muscle, a stomach muscle.'

'No.'

'Well, what have you done?'

'Nothing. Sarah, just leave me alone. I'll come inside in a minute and get cleaned up. Go and stop Ian getting Mrs Graff.'

'I can't.' Sarah sat on a flower pot opposite her friend. 'Grief, what's this?' She picked up a pillowcase.

'Don't know.'

'It's a pillowcase.'

'Don't be daft.'

'Mel, it is your pillowcase, see, the little flowers on it.'

'Violets.'

'Have you got your sleeping-bag as well?' Sarah thought out loud. 'Were you going to sleep out here? That doesn't make sense. Why bring your pillowcase and not the pillow? Mel, are you listening to me?'

'No.'

'What have you been doing? Agh, yuck.' Sarah had been fiddling with the pillowcase and had put her hand inside it only to meet the two remaining sticky buns. 'Mel, what's this?'

Mel was saved from answering by Ian's return. 'She's in the bath.'

'Who is?'

'Mrs Graff. Eleanor says, and Ivan the Terrible is on the prowl, checking up on where we all are. I came out of the dining room window,' Ian said proudly.

Sarah wasn't impressed. 'Well, go back in, bang on the bathroom door ...'

'Can't Eleanor do it?' asked Ian.

'Tell Eleanor about this and you're dead!' said Sarah.

'Some girlfriend you're turning out to be,' chuckled Ian. 'Okay. I've got the message. I'll go.' He turned to Mel. 'Are you better now?'

Mel got up. 'I'm fine.' The world spun round her head, so she sat down again quickly. 'I don't need Mrs Graff.'

'Ignore her,' said Sarah. 'Go.'

The two girls sat in awkward silence. Sarah had no idea what was happening to Melanie. Something was up and she wasn't going to leave her, whatever Mel said. She was bursting with a mixture of curiosity and concern and curiosity had the upper hand. A cold night, a leaky shed, buns in pillowcases, spilt milk, a pile of vomit and in the middle of it all, her best friend Mel, looking terrible. It was like a murder mystery on the television where they gave you all the clues but they don't make sense until the end of the programme.

'This doesn't make sense,' said Sarah, but Mel knew it did. Inside she felt dead. It was bad enough having to feed the lion regularly but this was even worse. She was going to be found out. God had let her down. He could have made Ian and Sarah walk the other way, but he hadn't bothered. He had done nothing to stop her bingeing either, and now he was going to make her look a fool unless she could think up a plausible excuse for why she was in this mess. God had let her down, Sarah had let her down. Her only hope was that Ian couldn't find Mrs Graff.

A dark shape appeared at the doorway. Mrs Graff stood there resplendent in unlaced walking boots, long thick dressing-gown, hair wrapped turban style in a towel, glasses steaming up and carrying a grey blanket.

'Ian says Mel is ill.'

'Yes,' said Sarah.

'No,' said Mel.

'Well, whether you're ill or not, Mel, you can't stay here.'

'I want to.'

The teacher's eyes quickly took in the details of the scene. Something odd was happening here. The girl had hardly eaten anything at all today, yet look at the heap of vomit! Now wasn't the time to investigate all this.

'Melanie. Bed,' she stated with authority.

'Mrs Graff, I don't think she likes the dorm,' Sarah knew that much. 'We've all been having a laugh about the triple bunks but Mel doesn't like them much.'

'No problem. Sarah, go and find one of the staff. There's bound to be someone still on duty. Ask them to open the sick room. It has got just two beds in it, ordinary ones, not bunks.'

'Yes, Miss.'

'And, Sarah, can you get Mel's sleeping bag and night things?'

'Her pillowcase is here. Dirty.'

'We'll find another one. Tell the others that she has got a bad stomach upset. I'll get her in the shower.'

Other people making decisions again but Mel didn't care. As long as no one found out what really happened, she would be safe. She showered, with Mrs Graff standing outside in case she felt dizzy, and then let herself be put to bed in the peaceful sick room, away from everyone else.

'Would you like Sarah or me to stay with you?' asked Mrs Graff.

'No, Miss.'

'Okay. There's a bowl here if you feel sick again. I suggest you have a few sips of water. I'll clean your Arran up, and, Mel, we'll have a good chat in the morning.'

'Yes, Mrs Graff. Thanks,' said Mel. 'A good chat'. Not on your life!

~ *13* ~

Mel lay awake for hours, trying to think how to get out of talking to Mrs Graff in the rapidly approaching morning. The best thing was just to listen and say no or yes at the right time. She could elaborate on the stomach upset theory but had no idea how to explain the buns, pillowcase or milk. Eventually she drifted off into a disturbed sleep.

Great sticky buns, like glacial boulders, pelted down at her as she tried to walk up a mountain in the pouring rain, only it wasn't rain, it was milk. Her waterproofs were made of pillowcases covered in violets, which were actually growing and threatening to strangle her with their whip-like tendrils. Distorted faces laughed at her, chanting 'Cain or Abel' and all the time she was trying to draw features of the landscape. Benjy appeared wearing Mum's Arran sweater, sitting on the back of Kevin's motorbike with Caroline, who was wearing Kevin's leathers and looked like a stick insect. As she chanted the past, present and future tenses of the French verb 'to go', the mountain turned into the sea and she walked into it, now wearing her bath towel. The rising bell startled her awake before she found out whether she drowned or not.

I'll get dressed and ready, as normal, Mel said to herself. Tell Mrs Graff I'm better and just lose myself in the group. As long as I stay with the others, she won't be able to talk to me. Anyway, there's nothing to talk about. We're leaving here at about four, so I've only a few hours to avoid her. She'll be so busy with her truncated spurs and glacial scree that she'll forget about last night. I'll skip breakfast so she won't see me.

There was a sharp knock on the door and Mrs Graff walked in followed by Sarah who was carrying a breakfast tray.

'What are you doing dressed? Now, back to bed this minute. Sarah's got you some tea and toast ...'

'And some for me,' said Sarah.

'So just take it easy and relax.' Mrs Graff opened the curtains. 'At least it has stopped raining.'

'I'm okay now,' began Mel.

Mrs Graff looked at her with disbelief.

'Really, I am.'

'Mel, no one is that sick and better a few hours later.'

'Perhaps I got rid of whatever it was in one go and I'm better now.'

'Perhaps. Anyway, Mel, you and I are staying here while the others go out until about three o'clock.'

'Can I stay, Miss?' asked Sarah.

'I don't think that will be necessary. You need to keep up with the work.'

'So do I, Miss,' said Mel. 'I'll get all behind. I won't be able to finish the work.'

'Mel, you are streets ahead. It'll not hurt you to miss a

few valleys and corrie lakes today. You can write anything else up from a textbook.'

'But I want to go!'

'No!' Firmly Mrs Graff took charge. 'You needn't get back into bed but I want you to take it easy and we'll have a chat later when I've got the others organised into their groups.' She moved towards the door. 'Sarah, please bring that tray down when you have finished.'

'Yes, Mrs Graff.' The teacher left and Sarah turned to her friend. Mel forced herself to eat a slice of cold toast, in case Sarah thought it odd if she didn't. She felt terribly guilty. Usually she half-starved herself after a binge, and did her sit-ups to try and flatten her stomach. She couldn't do anything like that with Sarah on guard.

'Eleanor thinks it was something in the tea in the café.'

'You've been talking about me! You promised.'

'Only about you being sick. I stopped Ian saying about the buns and your pillowcase.' Sarah looked pleadingly at her friend. 'What were you doing?'

'I told you, exploring.'

'I don't believe you.'

'That's your choice.'

'Well, I'm off.' Sarah put the crockery back on the tray. 'See you later. You know, Melanie Chambers, there are times when I wonder about you.'

You're not the only one, thought Mel. I wonder about myself all the time.

Despite hiding on an old settee at the back of the scruffy lounge, Mel was soon discovered by Mrs Graff. Everyone else had gone off in the minibuses and Mrs Graff looked quite relieved at not having to accompany them. She was carrying two earthenware pottery mugs full of hot coffee.

87

'Well, Mel, time for a little chat.' She pulled a chair round to face Mel. 'Before we start ...'

I'm starting nothing, thought Mel.

'I want you to know that anything you say to me will be treated as confidential. I won't talk to the other teachers, or your friends, or Janet, your mum, not unless you want me to. Do you understand?'

Mel nodded.

'I know I'm your teacher, but I've also known you, through your mum, since you were a little girl. I'm sure something is wrong. You've changed so much since last summer.'

'I've just grown up.'

'It's not that sort of change, Mel. You were always so full of life, now it is as if you want to get away, to withdraw. You seem afraid, scared of something.'

Of being found out, of the binges, thought Mel, squirming inside at the same time as sitting with a polite 'I am listening to you' look on her face.

'I'm sure it would help you to talk about whatever it is.'

'There's nothing.'

'I don't think that there's nothing. Melanie, what were you doing in a lean-to with a litre of milk, a pillowcase and, by the look of it, at least a dozen buns?'

'Nothing.' It had been nineteen buns, but she had left two.

'I don't think it was nothing.' Mrs Graff's voice was very soft. 'Melanie, I think you took the buns and milk, ate them quickly and then made yourself very sick. Am I right?'

'No.' Rising panic threatened Mel.

'I think I am, aren't I, Mel?'

'No!' The word was half-strangled.

'Melanie, please listen to me. It's the only explanation.

I think you've got an eating problem, an eating disorder. I don't think this is the first time this has happened. Am I right?'

Mel shook her head, seething with resentment, fear and the desire to run away.

'Lots of young people get eating disorders. I'm fairly sure you are not anorexic; you've got a lovely figure and you must be the right weight for your height. I think you've got bulimia. Do you know what that is?'

'Yes.' Course I know, it's when the lion takes over and screams to be fed and can only be shut up by being suffocated with food that then has to be got rid of. But I haven't got bulimia. That's what people in magazines get, and Princess Diana, and I'm not like that!

'It's a complicated thing, Mel, but you can get help.'

Mel sighed. 'Mrs Graff, I know you are only trying to be nice to me, but honestly you are worrying about nothing. I haven't got any disorder, eating or otherwise. I was just a bit sick.'

'On buns you hadn't eaten at tea! Melanie, the evidence is staring us both in the face. Why can't you admit it?'

'Because there is nothing to admit.' How dare you, Vicki Graff, make these accusations? How dare you say all this stuff about bulimia? I've got to cover up.

Mrs Graff tried once more. 'Bulimia is a sort of illness. If you had appendicitis, what would you do?'

'Go to the doctor. Probably have an operation.'

'Well, that's not much different to bulimia, except you don't need an operation. It can be helped. I'll not pretend it's easy but your doctor could start you on the road to recovery. There are specialists who deal with this sort of thing all the time. They can help. And, Mel, it can be dangerous.'

89

'Dangerous?' How could it be?

'A person with bulimia can have urinary infections which eventually lead to kidney failure, their teeth decay, their blood pressure increases.' Mrs Graff tried to remember what she had read on the Health Council's leaflet. 'Sometimes they haemorrhage and the balance of essential bits and pieces goes wrong. I think one of them is potassium.'

There was a long silence before she continued.

'And, Mel, I'm sure you know that bulimia is a way of dealing with difficulties in life, but it is not a good or safe way. We all have our problems. We all find ways of dealing with them, but bingeing and purging is not a lot of help in the long run.'

'I haven't any problems,' said Mel, in a quiet little voice.

Mrs Graff looked at her sadly. 'Haven't you, Mel, haven't you?'

For a moment Mel wanted to throw herself into Vicki Graff's arms and scream out, 'I'm bulimic, it's out of control, I can't stop it, I'm going mad, I don't know what to do! Help me, please, help me!' but she couldn't. Mrs Graff would be disgusted. Her parents would be horrified to find out that she wasn't the perfect daughter after all. No Chambers' daughter had problems, not ones they couldn't solve on their own, and her problem was too vile and repulsive to think about. Far better to pretend it didn't exist.

'Melanie, I can't make you talk. I can only pray that you will. I want you to know that it's okay to have a problem. It doesn't make you any less of a person. If you have bulimia, you have an illness, that's all. You're still Melanie, still special, still loved by God, still loved by others.'

90

Not if they find out, thought Mel.

'I want to help you, but it is up to you. No one can force you to do or be anything. You need help, Mel, but only you can decide that. I'm no expert – only you can choose whether or not to admit you have, or might have, an eating disorder. If you do want to talk, I want you to know I'm always available, at school, or at home. Okay?'

'Yes.'

'I need to clear up the study room. Why don't you get a bit of fresh air?'

'Good idea.' Mel pulled on a waterproof and went outside. She'd been found out. Mrs Graff knew. Her secret was a secret no more, but Mel had admitted nothing. It had really shocked her to be found out, but no one could prove anything. She was still safe. She would just have to work even harder at covering her tracks, but it was so difficult when the demanding lion was on the rampage.

~ *14* ~

Mel was silent on the coach journey home, hiding behind the non-existent stomach upset. Sarah had given up trying to talk to her. She was more engrossed in Ian, who had decided that although Sarah was pretty cool, her best friend was a bit loopy. Mel believed Mrs Graff would keep her word and not tell her parents. Apart from being told off about the state of the Arran jumper and listening to Mum's diatribe on the stupidity of leaving wellies in bushes, going home was something of a relief. At least at home she could time her binges so she remained undiscovered.

The next few days were spent avoiding as many people as possible and especially Mrs Graff. Mel imagined that her classmates were sitting talking about her, looking at her as she walked past. She was sure she could see the scorn and derision on their faces. They hated her, all of them. They knew she was repulsive. The only way to cope was to pretend that they did not exist, or to make-believe that she was invisible. Sarah tried to carry on being friendly, but by the Thursday her patience had worn thin. She had lent Mel her Geography notes, as hiding from Mrs Graff had meant missing her lesson.

'I don't know what you are up to,' said Sarah. 'What's Mrs Graff done to you? I covered up for you today, but she's not thick. She knows you are in school somewhere.' Mel had spent Geography leaning on the radiator in the girls' toilets. It had been the longest eighty minutes of her life.

'Just let me have the notes, I'll give you them back tomorrow.'

'I thought you two were friends, what with church and all that, and she was nice to you at the Field Centre. You've not got into trouble, have you, with being sick?'

'No.'

'Well, I don't know what game you are playing at but you can count me out. I can't cover up for you next week.' Mel decided to worry about next week another time. Sarah was becoming a real pain and Mel realised the only way to stop her incessant probing questions was to get her out of her life. On the one hand she needed Sarah's friendship so much, but on the other it was too dangerous. It was a chink in her self-protective armour, so Sarah would have to go.

'All you think about is Ian,' Mel lied. 'You've no time for me any more. I'm fed-up of you rabbitting on about him.'

'I've hardly said a word,' protested Sarah truthfully.

'Well, you two can keep up your pretty twosome and just leave me alone.' Mel hated saying the harsh words but she had no choice. 'Just get off my case, leave me alone, and get back to your precious boyfriend.'

Angry and hurt, Sarah snatched at her notes, which ripped dramatically, and stormed out of the loos. 'You know what, Melanie Chambers, you're a miserable, self-centred cow. I don't know why I've put up with you for so long.'

Mel locked herself into a cubicle and burst into tears. She so much wanted to run after Sarah, to apologise, tell her what was going on and get her friendship back. She couldn't. No one must know and to make matters worse the lion was waking up.

That evening Mel tried to write up her Geography from the glimpsed notes. She watched a bit of television with Granny who then went off to another meeting and she ignored Mum, who was stuck with her Psychology essay and muttering to herself. The lion was nearly awake but Mel knew she could ignore it. She took Benjy for a long walk, tiring both of them out, then she exercised for a while, weighed herself and measured her stomach, before being drawn to the kitchen, like metal to a magnet.

Mel had got to shut the lion up, but how? In her panic Mel opened containers in the pantry and thrust handfuls of whatever she could find down the chute to the lion. Raisins, cornflakes, brown sugar, a yoghurt, piece of stale bread, half a tub of glace cherries, some biscuits gone soft, great gulps of water, but it was nowhere near enough. She dare not take much of anything. Mum's latest attempt at a dairy and fat-free cake, which seemed to be mainly made of bran, sat cooling on the worktop. Mel tore a piece off.

'Melanie! Honestly! Use a knife. Whatever happened to your manners?'

'I'm just having a snack, Mum.'

'That's fine.' Mum looked puzzled. 'Why are all the tops off the containers? And the cupboard doors open?'

Mel improvised quickly. 'I was conducting an

experiment to see which were the most airtight.'

Mum smiled. 'Would you now conduct one to see which lid fits which container, and wipe up that sugar you've spilt.'

'Okay. I'm having a bath in a minute.' Mel went off, angry, unsatisfied, the lion still grumbling, her wits half-scared out of her by Mum's sudden appearance, to eject her 'snack' down the loo. She felt terrible. She was getting careless, but Mum didn't usually budge an inch when she was studying. All this secrecy and dodging people was exhausting.

Eluding Mrs Graff proved impossible the next day.

'Ah, Melanie, there you are,' she said casually at morning break. So casually that Mel had no idea how diligently Vicki Graff had been searching for her. 'Could I have a word?'

Mel knew better than to say no, so followed the teacher into a quiet corner of the dining-room. 'I've got Maths next, Miss.'

'I'm sure it won't matter if you are a bit late. I'll say I detained you.'

Mel's heart sank. This wasn't going to be a quick chat, then. Sweat broke out on the palms of her hands as she subconsciously pleated and unpleated her school skirt. She felt cold all over, vulnerable, exposed. Mrs Graff knew!

'Melanie, I'm not going through the "do you have a problem?" and "are you bulimic?" rigmarole again. That got us nowhere the other day, did it?'

Mel hung her head. Perhaps if she couldn't see Mrs Graff, she would go away. When Mel and Caro were little and played hide and seek, Mel would often hide her face under a cushion and then be annoyed when Caro easily found her. She felt like a little girl now.

'I've been reading up on eating disorders, Mel. I'm no expert but I believe that you have got a problem, a difficulty, and I want to help you.'

Mel remained quiet.

'I cannot help you to overcome the bulimia.'

Mel looked up at her then. Part of her wanted Mrs Graff to offer her an easy three-step miracle cure. What was the use of saying she wanted to help if she couldn't?

'However, I would love to support and encourage you, if only you'd be willing to face up to whatever is causing all this.'

'I don't know what's causing it.' Mel was unaware that her statement was admitting that she was in the grip of an eating disorder. Mrs Graff wasn't. Treading very carefully, like someone from the RSPCA trying to rescue an injured but frightened animal, she carried on in the same low-key tone of voice.

'There are people who are trained to help in all this, Mel. It would be wrong to mention names but you are certainly not the first girl in this school to suffer like this, nor, come to think of it, at church.'

'At church?'

'Yes, Mel, being a Christian doesn't make us immune from suffering.' A fleeting shadow crossed Mrs Graff's face as the image of her stillborn child and unfaithful husband of years ago came into focus. 'It's okay to have difficulties, things we can't deal with. In fact, I really believe that God wants us to use the help that is available, whether that is from friends or professionals, like doctors and therapists. A long time ago I needed lots of support when things were tough. I had to ask for help and I realised that there was nothing wrong with not being able to cope on my own. I'd like to support you now.'

'How?'

'I could come with you to tell Janet and Andrew.'

'Mum and Dad!' Mel was horrified. 'They must never know.' Quickly she changed track. 'Anyway, there's nothing to tell them, nothing for them to know.'

Mrs Graff continued, certain that Mel's confession had already been made. 'We'll tell your parents and then you can seek professional advice. First you go to your doctor and he will take it from there. You may be offered counselling or family therapy. I know Lu—' Mrs Graff just stopped herself from revealing the name, 'I know that's what happens sometimes.'

Family therapy! Mum! She must be joking. There was a long silence.

Something inside Mel started to change. It was as if a great solid block of ice had been brought into a warm room. Despite wanting to stay frozen, the ice had no choice. Slowly it started to thaw, tiny drips at the edges, which made miniature rivulets that Mel could not stop melting into uncontrollable streams.

'I can't. It's too hard, it's disgusting but I've go to do it,' she sobbed incoherently as Mrs Graff put her arms round her. 'The lion, I have to feed the lion, or it will destroy me. Sometimes it is anything, raw batter, cherries.'

'The buns?'

'Buns. Anything. It won't stop roaring, it hates me and I've got to shut it up until it goes away, and then I have to clean it up. Disinfectant, her foul shower gel, and it hurts, and I'm so fat and ugly and not like Caro and I'll never pass French.'

Mrs Graff held her quietly until the sobs subsided.

'I'm so scared. I'll never stop it. Never. I can't. Everyone hates me. I wish I were dead.'

'Melanie, please listen. There is a way through this. It'll be hard and painful, but no one can force it on you. Do you want to be free of all this – the lion thing?' Mrs Graff didn't know what Mel meant but the lion was obviously very important. 'The roaring, the eating, the being sick?'

'I don't know. Yes, of course I want to be different, but I can't. I can't do it. It's hopeless.'

'Melanie, there's always hope. There's professional help available. God loves you and knows what you are going through. He can give you the strength to battle with this. He accepts you, Mel, just as you are. He'll help you to cope and the professionals are very good. They deal with this all the time.'

Mel felt torn in half. She wanted to be free but she also wanted to hang on to the comfort of her twice weekly binges. She wanted to stop but there was no way she could tell her parents. She wanted to kill the lion but she might miss it. And what did all this have to do with those other things, the exam grades, being Caro's sister, going to university ... It was too confusing.

'Will you promise to think about it, Mel?'

'Yes, I will.' Mel felt more composed now.

'I know that it is difficult. It is up to you, Mel. I'm here to help but basically it is your choice. Do you want help or not?'

~ 15 ~

By Saturday morning Mel knew that she did not need help. She could crack this thing by herself. That way only Mrs Graff would know her shameful secret. Her parents would never need to find out. All she needed was a bit of will-power, to keep busy and then, in a few weeks' time, she could tell Mrs Graff that her problem was solved.

'Mum, I would like to make a special meal for tonight.'

'That's nice. What do you fancy doing?'

'I thought a proper beef roast. It's Dad's favourite and he's finished nights for a bit now, hasn't he?'

'It sounds lovely. You'll have to shop, though. There's some money in my purse.'

A joint of beef, sprouts, parsnips – Dad loved them roasted – horse-radish sauce, carrots, some eggs for a Yorkshire pudding, and all the wonderful ingredients for a fresh cream trifle. Mel made the list. She felt like she was testing herself. She could shop, buy nice things, cook them, eat a normal portion with the family, not be sick and that would prove that she was all right, that she could beat the bulimia, even supposing she had the bulimia in the first place.

The meal was a great success. Mel had persuaded Sarah to join them. Another test had been to phone up and apologise for her outburst in the loos.

'I must have gone nuts,' explained Mel. 'Everything got to me, but I'm fine now. I'm really sorry.'

'You were dead rude.'

'I know.'

'Anyway, I'll come about seven.' Sarah was spending the afternoon with Ian. It seemed wiser not to mention that.

Mel was delighted with the evening. She had done it. No binge, convinced Sarah she was normal, pleased her parents, amazed Granny, who had splashed rather runny trifle down her chest, and proved she hadn't a problem.

'That was wonderful, Mel,' said Mum. 'I've been thinking, though, that we should stop eating red meat. It is not so good for us.'

'Nor for the environment,' agreed Mel. 'It's such a long food chain.'

'It tastes good, though,' said Dad.

'So does chicken.' Mum had decided what the family would eat and Dad didn't bother arguing. Everyone knew who was boss in the Chambers' household. For once Mel felt no particular reaction to her mum. Nothing would spoil today and nothing did.

Mel and Sarah listened to music upstairs. Mel asked all the right questions about Ian and felt a genuine interest in her friend's love life. It was as if Mel wasn't Mel any more, almost as if she was floating above herself, watching herself, smiling at the right places, agreeing, nodding her head, feeling nothing except gratification that she was in control.

Well content, she spent a few minutes thanking God that she was okay now, as she snuggled into bed. In the distance a phone rang and moments later Mum came into the room.

'Mel, isn't it lovely! Caro is coming tomorrow, just for a few hours. Benedict is giving her a lift and picking her up later. It'll be lovely to see her, and I thought it would be Easter before she was home again.' Mum was rarely so excited. 'I thought you'd like to know.' She paused. 'Sorry, were you asleep?'

'No, Mum, it'll be good to see Caro. Night.'

However seeing Caro definitely wasn't good. Mel wasn't sure what it was but 'good' did not fit the whirlwind visit.

Benedict, a pale thin man with long blond hair, dropped her off in his new Rover car at eleven o'clock. 'See you later, Caro, darling,' he drawled.

'Is he your latest?' asked Granny, who had put on a clean dress, still flowery though, in honour of the occasion.

'Honestly, Grandmother, Benedict and I are just friends.' Since going to Oxford Caro had renamed everyone, including herself. She had always been known as Caroline up until then. Her mother and father seemed magnetised by her presence, like moths around a light. Mum, particularly, fed on her every word.

'Mother, this chicken is delicious but I do find that if you add a little more tarragon to the sauce, it brings out the piquancy.'

'I'll try that next time, Caro.'

'How are the studies?' asked Dad, and received a long

101

complex answer that no one understood.

'So you're still doing well?' he summed up.

Caro smiled patronisingly at him. 'Yes, Father. As long as I keep studying I think I'll be certain of a First.'

Mel and Granny cleared up, as Caro wasn't expected to on her visit home.

'Your sister is very clever,' said Granny, 'but where she gets her airs and graces from is beyond me. You're not like that.'

'I couldn't be if I tried,' said Mel.

'Well, my advice would be, don't try. That girl could learn a thing or two about how to treat other people.' She gave a surprisingly girlish giggle. 'What about Benedict then?'

'Benedict Thompson-Smythe?'

'The same one. Bet he's never washed a dish in his life. I don't know where she finds them.'

'She's very pretty.'

Granny looked at Mel. 'There's more to being attractive than a beautiful face, Mel. True beauty is from inside somewhere, but you're right, Caro is very pretty. Pity her attitude isn't so attractive.'

'I wish I was pretty.' Mel wasn't sure why she was confiding in Granny, but she just wanted to.

'Well, you needn't wish. You, my girl, are lovely. Don't you forget it.' Granny chuckled. 'Mind you, I'm biased.'

A voice called from the living-room, now called the lounge by Caro. 'Melanie, do come here. I've something for you.' Caro was delving into a large canvas bag. 'I don't need this anymore and I thought the colour would suit you.'

'This' was a beautiful, greeny patterned skirt. 'It's lovely, Caro,' said Mel. 'Thanks.'

Mum swiftly grabbed the skirt. 'It's a designer label,'

she said. 'Oh, Mel, it's a size ten, you'll never get in it.'

'It's quite a big ten,' said willowy Caro, stretching. 'I just thought it would look nice on you.'

'It would if she could get in it!' said Mum. 'Honestly, Caro, we can't all be like you. Do you know I've only lost two pounds since Christmas? At least the white meat has less fat.'

'Mel, you could leave the zip a bit open and wear a jumper with it,' suggested Caro, bored with the subject.

'Don't worry. I'll try to let it out,' said Mum. 'Such a shame to waste it. Are you sure you don't want it, Caro?'

'Mother, it's not my colour and Jeremy bought it for me and after his behaviour at the Christmas cheese and wine do, I never want to see him again.' And Caro embarked on a series of long, convoluted stories about who said what to whom.

Mel sat and watched. She felt the little self-confidence that she had was being fed into a shredder and ripped into thousands of small pieces that could never be put back together again.

It's not Caro's fault, she said to herself. I just wish I was her. Everything she does is better than me, she looks wonderful, she's so confident, she's not bothered about what other people think of her, she's never had a problem in her life. And boyfriends? Before Benedict and Jeremy there was that weird poet chap who never said a word, and the muscle-bound rower, Jordan, who was in love with himself, and a string of intellectual types. And does Caro care? Not a bit. She has a good time, gets bored, moves on to the next one and there's always loads of them waiting in line.

And me? No one. No one is the slightest bit interested in me. No boys, well, maybe Kevin. Not Mum, not Dad, Granny a bit but then she's nice to everyone. And Caro? I don't think she knows I exist. I'm never going to wear the skirt even if Mum makes it fit by a miracle.

In inner turmoil Mel sat and laughed and 'oohed' and 'you-nevered' at all the right places as Caro took centre stage and Mum enjoyed one of the best Sunday afternoons for ages. Caro even read through the Psychology essay and was full of praise. Mum actually glowed.

A horn tooted. Caro swiftly embraced them all, leaving her lingering perfume wrapped around Mel, and departed with Darling Benedict back to the dreamy spires and mellow stone colleges of Oxford.

It was as if someone had turned off an energy switch and the family sat quietly basking in the aftermath of Caroline's visit.

'That girl's too thin,' said Granny. 'And all this brain work will do her no good at all. She needs to get out into the real world now and then. That would knock a few edges off.'

Mum jumped to Caro's defence and she and Granny enjoyed one of their sparring matches. Dad and Mel went to church. Mel felt awful. The soaring success of yesterday was forgotten, erased from her memory. Now there was nothing but emptiness inside, hollowness that was going to demand to be filled.

In church Mel sat alone, standing and sitting at all the right places, avoiding catching Mrs Graff's eye. She had two pounds seventy-six pence, not even enough for a meal at McDonald's. How could she get enough food for the lion that was now on the alert?

'Dad, I'm going to coffee. After-Eights,' she told him.

'Okay, walk home with Sarah or someone.'

'Yes, Dad.' Mel went over to Sarah. 'Sarah, I can't come to After-Eights. I need to do a bit of work. See you tomorrow.'

Mel headed for the open-all-hours shop. 'Eight packets of biscuits, the cheap ones and a bottle of diet lemonade. I need them for the youth group, after church,' she explained to the shopkeeper. She hid the biscuits down the front of her coat, folding her arms across her chest to keep them in place, and walked to the park.

Swiftly Mel found her secret place near the holly bush and fir tree. It was very cold. Quickly she wolfed down the biscuits, faster and faster, forcing them down to her stomach with gulps of the over-bubbly lemonade. The panic that had been rising in her all day was halted. Mel waited to experience the welcomed, familiar wave of comfort and relief that made all this worthwhile. She was full, satiated with biscuits and pop, at peace for just a few moments. But the moments were getting fewer. The peace was being determinedly eroded by the stirrings of anger and disgust.

The vomiting left Mel tired and afraid as well as with a sore throat. This was hopeless. What had Mrs Graff said? Kidney failure. Mel didn't want to end up on a kidney machine. She didn't want to be ill.

She hated the stomach ache and the raw soreness of her throat when she was sick. She would never cope with kidney failure or those other things that could go wrong.

'I hate it,' she said out loud. 'I hate you.' The bulimia took on its own personality. 'Go away! Leave me alone! You've got to go away.' She cried. Mel had no idea how long it was before her sobs subsided. She hugged her knees, totally exhausted, as if every emotion, every ounce of energy, had drained out of her. It was no use. She couldn't handle it. 'Okay, I give up. I'll get help. I'll do anything, just leave me alone.'

~ *16* ~

First thing on Monday morning, Mel found Mrs Graff and asked if she could see her at lunch time. Last night had convinced Mel that she could not resolve her eating difficulties alone. She was worn out with the losing battles and knew that the longing to stuff herself to the point of bursting would sweep over her again and again.

Mrs Graff took her into a small study room where they would not be interrupted. She ripped a page off the calendar. February the second. The most miserable month in the year. Nothing could make Mel feel more miserable than she did now.

'Mrs Graff, I think I might have an eating problem. I don't know why. I don't understand it. I can't stop it and part of me doesn't want to stop it. I don't know what to do.' Mel spoke in an odd, flat voice, as if she was chanting her verbs.

Vicki Graff was so pleased that Mel had confided in her, but she deliberately spoke in a matter of fact voice. She had been reading about eating disorders and had spent Saturday afternoon with Lucy, the young woman from church who had nearly died from an infection contracted when she was dangerously anorexic. Lucy had made Mrs Graff realise that although she could offer Mel support, Mel must get medical, and probably, psychological help.

'I'm so glad you've told me, Melanie. It must have been very hard for you to decide to talk to me about it.'

'Not really, Miss,' and Mel poured out the story of the victorious Saturday and the dashed hopes of Sunday. 'I just can't control it. It is like a lion that lives inside me and when it wakes and wants feeding I have to do what it demands.'

'And what do you want to happen to the lion?'

'I want someone to kill it, now.'

Mrs Graff sighed. 'I wish it were that simple, Mel. Actually I think it might take a long time to get rid of the lion.'

'How long?'

'Months, maybe.'

'I can't go on like this for months!'

'I'm no expert, but I know you need to see your doctor, and get started on the road to recovery. It's a bit like taming a lion. It takes a long time to tame a wild animal, and I think your lion might be like that.'

Mel didn't know what to say. She had hoped for instant solutions.

'We need to tell your parents,' continued Mrs Graff.

'I can't.'

'Would you like me to come with you?'

'Can't you just see them on your own?'

'I don't feel that would be the best. Mel, hard as it is, you have to own this problem. You're nearly an adult, a young woman, it wouldn't be right for me to talk to

107

Janet and Andrew about you with you not there. I'll help you, give you all the support I can.'

'Well, can we do it soon, before I lose my nerve?'

'Tonight. They're in, aren't they?'

'Yes. Dad is back on days. Mum's not going out.' Mel dreaded the evening ahead. 'I can't do it.'

Mrs Graff reassured her and the break ended. Later Mel realised she must have phoned her parents at work. Mum wanted to know why her friend, and Mel's Geography teacher, was calling round at eight o'clock on a Monday evening, when she always went to her aerobics class then. Mel side-stepped her questions and hid in Granny's room, too worried to eat her tea, trying to block out the thoughts in her racing mind by watching television. She could not remember one item from the hour long national and local news programme, which Granny talked her way through.

Punctually at eight o'clock the doorbell rang and Mel, followed by Granny, who was determined not to miss anything, went down to the living-room. Mum was making a big deal out of pouring coffee into the best bone china mugs. Dad had been looking forward to an evening's viewing and wasn't too pleased with his wife's friend coming round on his first normal day's work in a month. Vicki Graff covered up her pounding nerves by smiling at Mel, who wished she was anywhere rather than here.

'Janet, Andrew, thank you for seeing me at such short notice. I won't beat about the bush, but Mel told me something today at school that I think you should hear.'

'She's not behind on her Geography project, is she, Vicki? I've seen the work she did for the Field Trip. It was good.' Mum was immediately on the defensive, talking about Mel as if she wasn't there.

'Her work is fine.'

'Well,' said Dad. 'I find it hard to believe that our Melanie is in trouble.'

'Mel's not in trouble ...'

Dad wasn't listening. 'I can't believe she's been smoking in the toilets, or giving cheek, or bullying or whatever goes on.'

Granny interrupted. 'Janet! Andrew! Listen, Vicki said it was something Mel told her. I think we want to know what it was, not get worked up about things she has not done.'

Good old Granny, thought Mel, whose courage had melted away.

'Well, tell us then, Melanie. What was so important that you had to tell Vicki, not me.' Mum's voice was ice-cold.

I can't, thought Mel, I can't say it.

'Melanie, I think it would help your mum and dad ...'

'And me!' said Granny.

'If you just told them what you told me, and,' she glared at the other adults, 'we'll all keep quiet until you've finished.'

'I can't,' whispered Mel. 'I can't.'

Mrs Graff put her arm round her shoulder. 'Mel, you've got the strength to do this, please.'

'I didn't know how to tell you, but Mrs Graff said I must, to get started on stopping.' The family looked totally bemused. 'So, I've written it out.' Mel took a piece of well-folded paper out of her pocket and began to read. 'I think I have an eating disorder. I think it is called bulimia. I've tried to stop it and I can't.' She paused. Worse was to come. 'About twice a week I get as much food as I can, loads of it and eat it very quickly. Then I make myself sick, about ten times, until all the

109

food has gone.'

Mel stopped. Her prepared statement had ended abruptly. She hadn't known what else to say so had said nothing. There was a stunned silence, then Mel felt what was left of her tiny world was smashed to pieces as everyone spoke at once.

'Don't be so stupid! You're just being hysterical. Vicki, how could you believe this garbage?' Mum was mad.

'What's she mean, being sick ten times?' Granny was confused.

'I don't believe it,' said Dad.

'There's nothing to believe!' Mum again. 'I'm shocked at you, Vicki. How could you put these ideas into her head? I've never seen her sick.'

'Have you got a stomach ulcer, or one of those hernia things?' asked Granny. 'You want to take milk of magnesia or peppermint cordial, that'll settle your stomach.'

Mum rounded on her mother. 'You old fool. She's not saying she's got a flaming ulcer, she says she makes herself sick.'

'All fibs,' said Dad. 'Really, Melanie, what a fuss about nothing.'

'It isn't nothing.' Vicki Graff came to the rescue. 'It's true.'

'True, my foot! You're a teacher, not an expert in bulimia! And, Melanie, I think you should go to your room until you've put these silly ideas out of your head,' said Mum.

'No.'

'No?' Mum wasn't used to defiance. 'No?'

'No. Mum, I haven't made it up.'

'You must have.'

'No, Mum, it's true. I binge. I'm sick.'

'Melanie, everyone is sick sometimes, or eats too

110

much.' Mum tried to laugh. 'Look at me, two helpings of that lovely trifle you made on Saturday. That doesn't mean I have an eating disorder.'

'Janet, Melanie's not talking about double portions of pudding,' said Vicki Graff. 'She's talking about a problem, a real problem, like an illness.'

'My girls have never had a day's illness in their lives!'

'Measles, chicken-pox, that 'flu bug last year, and which one got the mumps really bad when they were five?' Granny counted the illnesses off on her fingers.

'Shut up, Mother!'

'Janet, it's not that sort of illness, but Melanie needs to see your doctor, to get help.' Mrs Graff could see why Mel could never have faced her parents alone.

'But there's nothing wrong. Look at her. She's a lovely girl, not in Caro's league, I admit.' The thoughtless words sliced like a sword into Melanie's heart, stirring up a dormant volcano of anger which spewed over into an uncontrollable lava flow, burning down Mum's adamant denial of there being any problem.

'Remember the Weetabix? I ate them, seventeen of them, along with half a pound of butter and a pack of cheese. And the loaf you defrosted? In one go, in the loft.'

'The loft?' Dad was totally lost.

'I spent ten pounds on food at PriceRight the other week, when you were at Psychology, and ate the lot in twenty minutes. Last night it was eight packs of biscuits.'

'Melanie, stop.' Mrs Graff tried to stem the flow.

'So don't you dare tell me I haven't a problem. Don't you dare,' and Mel ran out of the room and locked herself in the bedroom.

From downstairs she could hear Mum's angry raised voice, Dad's occasional comments, Granny's mutterings and Vicki Graff's controlled words. Doors slammed. There was shouting. Mel heard Granny's slow footsteps on the stairs.

'So you say it's not my business! Janet Chambers, I'm ashamed of you. You've pushed that girl far too much, you and your precious education.'

'Mother, you're not helping,' came Mum's voice up the stairwell.

'Neither are you!' Granny reached her bedroom sanctuary. Downstairs the voices became more muffled and after an absolute age there was a knock on the bedroom door. It was Dad.

'Melanie, we would really appreciate if you would come downstairs, just for a few moments. Please. No one will shout.'

Reluctantly Mel followed him back to the living-room. Dad seemed to be spokesperson, which was unheard of. Even in her distress, Mel registered her amazement at the way he was taking control. It's probably because Mum has gone to pieces, thought Mel.

Mum had obviously been crying, mascara smudged over her cheeks and looked like a whipped animal cowering at the back of her armchair, chewing her knuckles. Vicki Graff's face was tear-blotched as well. Mel felt like a disinterested spectator at a disaster, her anger spent, too exhausted to identify emotions that were occurring within her.

'Melanie, we've been talking. I'm sorry that we did not take you seriously when you told us about your problem. Thank you for telling us.' Dad was standing up talking stiffly, making the longest speech Mel could ever remember. 'Vicki has told us about bulimia and apparently what we need to do is to get you to Doctor Ferrars as soon as we can. Then we can take it from there.'

Turning to look straight at her he continued. 'I don't understand any of this, Melanie, neither does your mother.' Mum looked as if she might pass out at any minute. 'But we are committed, both committed, to helping you get over this. So, Melanie, would you be willing to go to see Doctor Ferrars?'

'Yes, Dad.' Mel felt the tiniest stirrings of hope. Dad had asked her if she would go to the surgery. He hadn't told her, hadn't insisted, but asked. Mel couldn't imagine Mum ever doing that.

'So, I'll make us an appointment?'

'Us?'

'We'll all go and see what he says.'

'Okay, Dad, can I go now?'

'Of course.' Dad walked across the room and gave her a sudden hug. Melanie couldn't remember when he had last done that. She stood still, clenching her fists, not knowing how to respond. 'We love you very much, Melanie.' Mum said nothing.

'Yes, Dad. Goodnight,' and Mel dragged her drained body off to the safe haven of bed. What a night!

~ *17* ~

Visiting the doctor was only the beginning of a long and hazardous journey for Mel. At his suggestion the family decided to accept family counselling. The process was very painful for all of them.

Mel was not aware of what had started her out on the bulimic road and she had thought that she would be given a few exercises to help her change her eating habits and to increase her self-control. However it was not like that. Sometimes the therapist would see her on her own, at other times with Dad and Mum, and still others just with Mum. Very slowly Mel began to realise that her eating disorder had developed as a way of dealing with the things in her life that she found it hard to think about, let alone talk about.

Every week Doctor Repton, a kind, surprisingly motherly figure, would try to get Mel to talk about herself. At first it was just too difficult. No one had ever before particularly wanted to know what Mel felt and thought, yet Doctor Repton acted as if it was the most important thing in the world. Half the time Mel did not know what her emotions were, or whether she really had them, but patiently the therapist drew her out. Mel found herself able to tell stories from her childhood, from recent years, from these last awful months. She could not see any connection with the bulimia, but gradually trusted the therapist and believed she knew what she was doing.

It seemed almost wicked to start to talk about how she felt about life, about her family and about her needs. All her life Mel had never been free to acknowledge her thoughts and wishes. So often her needs had not been met, but Mel blamed herself for that. How could they know what effect they had on her if she never told them? How could she talk of jealousy, of feeling inadequate, of never being quite good enough and then spoil the ideal family? How could she have ever been anything but the good girl who never caused anyone any trouble and who was a credit to her family?

The questions inside her head tormented her, and slowly feelings and emotions that had been buried alive began to bubble to the surface like the gases from putrifying flesh. Mel was frightened with their intensity and wanted to bury them again, deeper and deeper, until they suffocated, but she could not. She admitted that at times she had hated Caroline, the ever-shining example held up to her. She had covered up her frustration with Mum's control of her life by being compliant, doing what she was told, never causing a fuss and striving to meet Mum's impossible expectations of her.

Mel had to face up to her relationship with her mum. It was the worse part. Racked with guilt, it took weeks before she could whisper to Doctor Repton that she felt furious rebellion against her mother and real anger that

God had landed her with such a parent. Repeatedly Mel excused her mother's controlling behaviour, putting all the blame for their uneasy relationship upon herself. After all Caroline didn't have this problem and they had the same parents.

The therapist kept on probing, spilling more and more emotions out of Mel. From tentatively identifying anger, Mel was able to see that she also experienced fear, shame, disgust, jealousy, hatred, panic and depression as well as love and glimpses of hope. Encouraged to keep a mood and food diary, Mel began to see that there might possibly be a relationship between how she dealt with her emotions and what she believed she had to eat. She remained unconvinced that she was at an ideal body weight.

They talked about the lion a lot. It still got hungry. Sometimes Mel could send it away. Sometimes she had to satisfy its greed. After a binge-purge episode Mel would try to write down what had happened and, with the therapist's help, learn what triggered the attacks. Doctor Repton encouraged her to see these binges as temporary lapses but they didn't feel temporary to Mel. The lion might be being tamed but at times it still went on the rampage.

Mum was finding all this process dreadful. Her pre-conceptions were being challenged. Her whole way of thinking was under the microscope. One minute she was blaming herself totally for Mel's difficulties, the next she refused to believe they were in any way related to her. She tried to re-examine her attitudes to academic success but they were so deeply ingrained in her, it was nearly impossible. With visible reluctance she let Mel drop French and Music, even though the final exams were in sight. Forcing herself, she tried to talk to Mel about her own feelings and to get Mel to talk back.

Mel found it so hard. Sharing what she was thinking was just about possible, but feelings were another matter. It was better if Dad was present. He had realised that he had been in danger of losing his relationship with his daughter by his near obsession with his family tree. He was able to switch his energies to trying to get to know Mel and soon found out that it was going to be as painstakingly erratic as researching ancestors.

After a medium binge, when Dad heard Mel retching, Mum put padlocks on all the cupboard doors and even fixed a huge bolt affair on the fridge. Mel was distraught.

'You don't trust me,' she said, when Dad had come home. 'Do you?'

Mum's face gave the answer. 'I'm only trying to help you, Melanie. I thought if I locked the doors, you wouldn't be able to get to the food, and you couldn't binge.'

'But, Mum, don't you see. You are doing it again.'

'Doing what?'

'Making choices for me. Taking away from me the right to make decisions, even the right to binge.'

'Right to binge!' Mum was getting annoyed. 'I thought the whole point of all this, the therapist, the family counselling, was to stop you bingeing.'

To Mel's surprise, Dad intervened. Mel still wasn't used to him being in charge. 'Janet, calm down. Now you know what Doctor Repton says. Melanie must take personal responsibility for her problem.' He quoted. 'I'm sure she knows your motives are good, but I think we'll just take these locks away, don't you agree?'

'Do as you like.'

Mel watched as Mum slumped in a chair. All at once she realised that in some ways this was as hard for Mum

117

as it was for her. She had had sixteen years to get like she was, but Mum had had nearly fifty. No wonder it was so hard for her to change. For the first time Mel felt pity for her mum, struggling with something she did not understand.

Vicki Graff had been great, supporting them all. From Mel's point of view the best thing she had done was to introduce her to Lucy, the young woman from church who had nearly died from anorexia. Through Lucy she got to know other people with eating disorders and the five of them would get together to encourage each other. Melanie had thought Lucy, who had not been able to face food, would be disgusted at herself, who had swallowed basketfuls. She need not have worried. Lucy was great. She listened, she cared and often, when Mel felt compelled to binge, she would phone Lucy up and go round to her flat.

Mel told her how she struggled with God about the bulimia. 'I asked him to stop me, and he didn't. He could have made me so I never started in the first place, but he didn't. He's so confusing. When I was in Wales, in the shed,' Lucy knew all the details, 'I pleaded with him to not let me be found out, but I was. He just doesn't answer my prayers.'

Lucy, still angularly slim, leant forward. 'So he doesn't answer your prayers?'

'No.'

'And you asked him to stop the bulimia?'

'Yes.'

'And for you not to get caught bingeing or being sick?'

'I told you, yes.'

Lucy continued thoughtfully. 'Has it ever occurred to you, Mel, that he did answer your prayers?'

'How?

'Vicki Graff.'

'Mrs Graff? Why?'

'If she hadn't surprised you, in Wales, what would have happened?'

'Well, nothing, I suppose.'

'And because she found you, what happened?'

'She wouldn't get off my case.' Mel's face lit up. 'Then I wouldn't have admitted I had a problem and I wouldn't have started to get help.'

'So maybe God did hear you, Mel. I wonder if he answered your real prayer, the one about sorting out the bulimia, not the one about being discovered.'

'You might be right,' admitted Mel. 'That makes sense, but why did I get bulimia in the first place?'

'And why did my weight go below five stones? I don't know, Mel, why some of us are prone to these things, why we choose food as our way of coping with life. Perhaps we'll never know.'

'So are you saying we just have to trust that God knows why we're like we are.'

'Something like that. You know, Mel, the biggest thing I learnt through it all is that God loves me as I am. I don't need to have control of my life by not eating food. I can be whatever's the right weight for me.'

'I can't say all that,' said Mel.

'I wouldn't expect you to. Mel, I'm nearly ten tears older than you. I started getting treatment five years ago, and I still sometimes get into a state. You've only been getting help since February.'

'But I want to be okay now.' Mel stated. 'It's taking so long.'

'I know, but you'll make it in the end, Mel, I know you will. I pray for you every day and so do other people.'

'But I still binge sometimes.'

'The 'sometimes' will get less.' Lucy said. 'Who knows. in five years' time you might help someone else.'

'And pigs might fly!' Mel found Lucy such a good friend, even more help at times than Doctor Repton.

The weeks wound on. Mel had told Sarah and, after lots of questions, she had proved to be a really good friend. No one else at school knew, not even Ian. Sarah sat with Mel every lunch break making sure she ate her meal, mothering her, until Mel stopped her.

Therapy continued. There was one horrendous binge when Mum had been going on about Caroline. Mel stole a ten pound note from her purse and escaped to the park with her gateau, cakes and ice-cream to deaden the pain. However, she managed to confess and Mum actually thanked her for being honest, which was a bit odd, when she had stolen the money. Mel's therapist had taken two sessions to talk through that episode. At night Mel would lie in bed, contemplate her body, wish she was thinner, be glad she wasn't anorexic and make herself talk to God. She would tell him about the day's events, how she had felt, whether she had wanted to binge or not, if she had binged. Then Mel would make an imaginary parcel of the day and place it into God's hands. At peace, she would drift off to sleep, the day's successes and failures given to someone else.

~ 18 ~

It was a glorious hot day near the end of June and the exams were over. No matter what anyone did now it would make no difference to the final results. No more studying. No more soil moisture meters that would not work. No more essays and assignments, projects and revision. It was all over.

Melanie's classmates decided to celebrate by going out together for a pizza. They had been together for at least five years, and now some were going their different ways. Tina was going to work for a nursery until she could do her nursery nurse training. Liz had a job in a travel agency. Mel and Sarah wanted to stay on at the Sixth Form College attached to the school, while others were waiting for their results before they decided what to do. The future seemed unimportant. What mattered now was that the exams were finished.

'I don't think I can go,' said Mel to Sarah, as they talked about the meal out. 'I haven't been out for a meal since before Christmas.'

'I know, Mel, but you'll be okay.'

'Sarah, I still have to be careful. What if something triggers me off? What if I lose control in front of everyone? No one but you knows about the bulimia.'

'Mel, how long is it since your last binge?'

Mel thought. 'It was after the second Science paper. The one I thought I had messed up, so it must be, let's see, nearly three weeks.'

'That's brilliant. It's the longest yet.'

'But Sarah, the lion might wake up. I don't know if it has gone yet.'

'Well, talk to Doctor Repton about it, or that Lucy you see. You've got to come. It won't be the same without you.'

'Won't it?'

Sarah did not bother answering straight away. Mel knew the answer. That was one thing that Mel was beginning to believe about herself. She was a person, she was important to some people, like Sarah and Mum and Dad. Even Caro had been nice to her lately. Despite being in the middle of her Finals at Oxford, she had sent Mel a funny Good Luck card for the exams and had phoned to chat just to her at least once a week. And Granny fussed and clucked over her all the time.

Sarah finally answered. 'It won't be so much fun without you.'

'I'll come. See you later.' Sarah couldn't have said anything better to persuade Mel to go. Her friends were starting to think she was fun again.

They had all decided to dress up smartly for the visit to the pizza place which was rather different, as usually Mel's friends visited the restaurant in jeans and T-shirts. Now her allowance wasn't all going on food, Mel had saved up and bought herself a floaty summer dress. Sarah had tried to get her to buy a fitted mini-skirt, but Mel was not yet confident enough to show off her figure. She felt her legs were still too fat above her knees and her stomach too rounded, but when she put the new dress on, even Mel realised she looked good.

'Wow,' said Dad. 'You'll turn a few heads tonight.' He gave her some extra money for the meal.

'Mel, do be careful, the desserts, chocolate ...' Mum was fretting.

'Janet, she'll be fine. Personal responsibility, remember.' Dad shut her up. 'Mel, did you take Doctor Repton's advice?'

'Yes, Dad. I ate lunch with Mum and I had a piece of toast and some fruit about six so I wouldn't be starving tonight. I'll be okay.'

'I know you will.' Dad looked as if he meant it. Mum couldn't quite hide her lack of conviction. 'I'll give you and Sarah a lift if you like. Save getting the bus.'

'Thanks, Dad, but don't pick us up afterwards. If it is really late we can share a taxi.'

Granny insisted on coming for the ride and Mel had to be firm with her to stop her coming into the restaurant to have a look at what all her classmates were wearing.

Mel felt happy and excited. The meal was a great success. Eleanor was taking photos of them. About twenty of them were crammed either side of a load of small tables that had been pushed together. Sarah made sure she sat next to Mel and that Tina was on the other side with Liz, Eleanor and David opposite. They did not know about the bulimia but they did know that Mel had been through a hard time, rumoured to be stress about the exams. Sarah thought they would be nice to Mel and they were.

She was glad she had Ian on the other side of her. It had been really difficult not telling him about Mel's condition, and Sarah hoped Mel would let her inform him soon. She hated having secrets from Ian, who had told her she worried too much about her friend. Often Ian, Sarah and Mel spent an evening together, supposedly studying at Sarah's house, but often joined by Kevin. Sarah was sure Kevin fancied Mel but wasn't sure what Mel thought. She did not know if she wanted her brother to go out with her best friend. With all her imagination she could not conjure up what Mel would be attracted to in Kevin, but Sarah had a growing suspicion that she was.

The starters and first course passed without incident. Huge bubbling pizzas and plates of salad had been consumed when the dessert menu was produced.

'Alabama mud pie for me,' said Eleanor.

'Toffee fudge gateau,' said David. 'Bet you'll have that, Ian?'

'No, I'm going for the Death by Chocolate!' Ian rolled his eyes and pretended to gasp his last breath. 'How about you, Sarah? If you have the Black Forest gateau, we can share halves each.'

Sarah felt a frantic tug on her hand. It was Mel, who was starting to feel panic. She would love to eat all of those wonderful desserts but she dared not. Mel knew that even a few mouthfuls of creamy chocolate could trigger a binge and she felt trapped. They would make her order one and she wouldn't be able to not eat it and then what would happen?

Sarah realised some of what was racing through Mel's mind. She remembered that desserts were still a big problem. Longing for a scrumptious piece of the mud pie, she made a decision.

'I'm going to have the fresh fruit salad.'

'What a bore! You can have that anytime,' protested Ian.

'Well, it's what I want this time.' Sarah turned to Mel, trying to send a message that said she understood what was going on. 'What about you, Mel?'

'I'll have the same as you, Sarah. I'm really full.'

'Well, I'm not having any wimpy fruit salad,' said Tina. 'Double chocolate mousse for me.'

'Remember when we made mousse in cooking, in year nine, I think?' said Sarah, trying to redirect the conversation. 'My eggs wouldn't whip up, David dropped his and Ian's mousse looked like sludge by the time he'd finished.'

Tina joined in. 'My mum went mad. She said it was far too expensive to make and a stupid thing to be trying to cook.'

'I remember she wrote to the school. After that we had to do boring things, like pastry,' added Liz.

'Remember David's scones? They sank without trace when we took them to feed to the ducks after school.'

'And you got so mad, David, you fell in.'

'You're always falling in water, David. The Glaslyn in January ...'

David interrupted, 'That was freezing. I was really scared.'

Eleanor, who had slipped in the Glaslyn with him, looked surprised. 'You never said so at the time. You said,' she tried to remember, 'that it was nothing for a man who was going to cross the Antarctic single-handed one day.'

'So we called you Antarctic Dave for weeks,' said Liz.

'Or Penguin,' said Mel, joining in. 'You never said you were scared.'

'Well, I was,' replied David. 'I bet even you, Melanie Chambers, get scared sometimes.'

Mel looked straight at him. 'Of course I do. You'd be amazed at what I get afraid of.'

'Like what?'

'Like not passing exams, messing things up,' said Mel. Like the lion waking from hibernation, said a little voice inside her.

'You! Worried about exams!' Liz was incredulous. 'If anyone will get good grades it'll be you.'

'It doesn't stop me being afraid,' explained Mel. 'Also, I still don't know what I want to do for 'A' levels. That can make me feel quite insecure.' Mel could hardly believe that not only was she resisting chocolate desserts, she was also telling her friends what she thought and felt.

'I wonder if your Kevin knows there's more to Mel than meets the eye,' said Ian, in a stage-whisper to Sarah.

'What's Kevin got to do with anything?' Mel blushed bright red. 'He's not even at school.'

'Ah, what's he got to do with anything at all?' said Sarah, mysteriously, enjoying herself. 'I think we might find out more over the summer, eh, Ian?'

The two of them started laughing. Ian choked on his Death by Chocolate, took a swallow of his coke, spluttered and gasped as the bubbly drink shot out of his nose and onto the new white shirt he was wearing. Everyone roared with laughter. Young ladies in smart dresses forgot they were adults and started flicking bits of food across the tables, while the young men made paper darts out of napkins.

At that point the management intervened firmly. Coffee would be served at the celebratory party if missiles were dismantled and the noise level reduced by fifty decibels. There were other people in the restaurant.

A hush fell, the debris of the meal was cleared up, coffee was served. David decided to be master of ceremonies and rose to propose a toast with the remains of his coke:

'To year eleven: may God bless her, and all who sail in her.' He liked films about naval battles and his latest idea was to become a ship's captain.

'To year eleven.' The classmates stood up, clinked assorted glasses and cups and sat down as the general hubbub of noise increased.

Mel sat quietly, watching the scene. She was trying to work out what she would write in her mood and food diary tonight. She smiled. For the first time since she began to keep the diary she could record an emotion that she thought she had lost for ever. Happy.

Tonight Melanie Chambers was happy. She was one of the crowd, accepted. It didn't matter whether she was clever, average or slow. Her friends liked her. Sarah was a great friend to have. Mel had eaten a big meal and didn't feel compelled to vomit it up in the toilets. She had resisted desserts that could trigger a binge. Mel even felt warm towards Mum, who was still often a pain to live with. She knew that tomorrow everything might feel different, but tonight she was happy and enjoying the unfamiliar emotion that she hoped would one day be a constant companion.

If after reading this book, you would like more information and help concerning eating disorders, you can contact:

Anorexia and Bulimia Care (ABC), 15 Fernhurst Gate, Aughton, Ormskirk, Lancashire. L39 5ED.
Tel: 01695 422479
Anorexia and Bulimia Care is a Christian organisation offering help to sufferers of eating disorders through a network of carers. You can send for further information, a 'starter pack' and a magazine called *Lifeline*.

Eating Disorders Association (EDA), Sackville Place, 44 Magdalen Street, Norwich, Norfolk. NR3 1JU.
Youth helpline tel: 01603 765 050 (4–6pm, Mon–Fri)
EDA is a national charity which offers information and help to people with anorexia and bulimia.
If you need to talk to someone, you can ring the EDA youth helpline. All calls are confidential, and the EDA counsellor can ring you back to save you the cost of the telephone call.

BY THE SAME AUTHOR

Secret Never to be Told
Cathie Bartlam
Karen tells Abi she has been sexually abused and swears her to secrecy. Abi struggles to accept that God could let this happen – and her doubts affect her own behaviour and relationships.

Price £3.25